WALKER REVENGE

BERNADETTE MARIE

5 PRINCE PUBLISHING

5 PRINCE PUBLISHING

PO Box 865 Arvada, CO 80001

www.5PrinceBooks.com

ISBN Digital: 978-1-63112-180-7

ISBN Print: 978-1-63112-181-4

WALKER REVENGE. Bernadette Marie

Published by 5 Prince Publishing

Cover Credit: Bernadette Soehner

First Edition September 2016

5 PRINCE PUBLISHING AND BOOKS, LLC.

❀ Created with Vellum

For Stan,
Grateful that you've always had, and will always have, my back!

ACKNOWLEDGMENTS

To Stan who has always had my back—no questions asked.

To my boys who have no idea how much they protect one another, even when they've had enough of one another.

To my parents and my sister, I thank you for always being there when I need(ed) you.

To Clare and Cate, thank you for jumping in with both feet and understanding me, even when sometimes I don't know what the heck I'm doing.

To my street team, thank you for your love and support. I enjoy writing stories for you all.

Dear Reader,

I am thrilled to bring you Russell Walker's second chance romance story. As we've learned, Russell is perhaps the Walker most likely to get into a fight, as is the case in this story. However, in a happily ever story, we also know, that means he's a softy deep inside.

I find, being such a passive aggressive person, I enjoy writing men with a little bit of an attitude, and the women who can give them a run for their money. Perhaps it's a bit of therapy for me.

I hope you'll enjoy this installment to the Walker family.

Happy Reading,
  Bernadette Marie

WALKER REVENGE

CHAPTER 1

$\mathcal{D}$aytime TV sucked. If he was subjected to one more game show or stupid talk show, Russell thought he might just throw the remote control through the front of the TV.

There was only one upside to being laid up in a hospital bed—bedside food delivery.

"You look like crap," his brother's voice came from the doorway.

When Russell turned he saw Dane standing there, but the look on his face wasn't one of humor, as the comment might have suggested. He looked mortified.

"Why'd you leave your vacation so soon?"

"Italy is ugly. Thought this would be a better use of my time." Dane stepped into the room and looked down at the tubes and bandages that encompassed the lower left side of Russell's body. "What the hell happened?"

Russell ran his hand over his stubbly chin, dragging wires and tubes along with his hand. "I got pinned in my truck."

"Mom said you flipped it."

Russell pursed his lips. Admitting fault wasn't something he was particularly good at. He was better at dealing with things in a physical manner.

"Hence me getting stuck in the freaking truck."

Dane rubbed his eyes. "I see it did a number on your attitude too."

"Did you come here to fight with me?" He heard his words slur from the crap they'd knocked him out with. Why did that stuff have to stay in a body so long? "What the hell time is it anyway?"

"Six in the morning."

Russell turned off the TV. "And here I thought I was watching crappy daytime TV. I guess it's just always bad." He winced from the pain that seemed to be greater than the pain medicine pumping through his IV. "Why are you here at six in the morning?"

Dane moved to the chair next to the bed. "I flew in and came straight here."

"You left Italy to come here? Dude, I'm sorry."

Dane grinned. Maybe he sounded worse in reality than Russell thought he did in his own head.

"You're sorry? I never thought I'd hear you say that."

"How did it go?" He wasn't in the mood to be jabbed at.

Dane's expression changed and his eyes lit up. "It's a beautiful place. It'll be nice when I go back."

"You're going back?"

"Sure we will. That's where Gia's from. Besides, she wants to honeymoon in Paris."

Russell tried to sit up but found it took too much effort. "Honeymoon? What the hell is that supposed to mean?"

"She proposed to me," Dane said, and the smile on his mouth was enormous. The urge to slap it off surged through Russell.

"She proposed to you? You couldn't even do that right?"

Dane shrugged. "You know me. I would have waited too long."

Russell felt the quick fatigue of arguing with his brother begin to take over. He batted his eyes against it.

The next time he opened them the room was quiet. Faint light pushed through the drawn shade, and a woman stood next to him. He smiled through the haze he was feeling.

She was holding his hand in her hands. Blonde strands of hair hung around her face, but the rest was piled up in a messy bun atop her head.

This was familiar, he thought as he took a cleansing breath and then wiggled his nose because his nasal cannula was making it itch.

"I didn't mean to wake you. I was just getting your vitals," her voice was soft and oh so familiar.

"What time is it?" His voice was barely functioning.

"Just past eight."

"I was talking to Dane."

She laughed now, and that, too, was familiar. "He left hours ago. He looked as though he needed some sleep. Pretty exciting that he's getting married to Gia. I enjoy her store."

That danced around in his head, and so did whatever they'd put into his IV, but at least he wasn't in any pain.

"You know Gia?"

"Of course, I do."

Russell lifted his hand, cords and all, and rubbed his eyes. He wasn't seeing clearly, and his mind was beginning to play tricks on him.

Now he turned his head so he could better see the woman in the dimly lit room. Her head was hung as she focused on reading the monitor at his side, but he knew the curves of her face.

He'd heard that dreams could be vivid when you were on pain meds. Seriously that had to be what was happening.

"Chelsea?" Her name seemed louder when he said it, but she lifted her head.

"Hello, Russ."

She went back to looking at the monitor. "What are you doing here?"

"I went back to school." She lowered his arm back to the bed and then pushed a few buttons on the machine. "How are you feeling?"

"Fine. Confused. You're a nurse?"

"Nursing student. I'm being supervised, so please don't argue with me."

This was no dream. She was already mad at him and he'd only said a few words to her.

Russell reached for her, and she quickly glanced out the window used for observation. "What can I do for you, Mr. Walker?"

"Stay for a little bit. I'd like to talk."

"I have rounds to make. I can't spend any time in here talking. If you'd be more comfortable, I could ask to be transferred to another unit."

His world was fuzzy again, but he wasn't done. "No, I don't want that at all. I owe you an apology. I want to give that to you."

She turned to the computer at his bedside, scanned her ID tag, and then entered something with her back turned to the window.

"Russ, I hate to see you in here like this, but something tells me you deserved it."

"That's a horrible thing to say."

She gave him a grunt. "You got in a fight at a bar before you flipped your truck because you'd been drinking."

"I wasn't drunk," he defended.

"Maybe not, but your mouth was getting you in trouble, which says to me, nothing has changed." She tucked one of those loose strands of blonde hair behind her ear, a sign that she was nervous. "If you're sincere about talking, I'll come back when my shift is over."

"I'd like that," he said, but his tongue felt as though it filled his mouth and didn't sound right. "I'm sorry," he said slurring his words.

"We gave you something to manage your pain. You will probably sleep a lot."

His eyelids grew heavy again, but he forced them back open. "I love you, Chelsea," he managed before he couldn't open them again.

CHELSEA FOCUSED on the computer screen, or pretended to. In her month of internship at the hospital, she'd run into a lot of people she knew. She'd never thought she'd run into Russell Walker, at least not in the shape he was in.

She glanced at him from the corner of her eye. He was smiling in his sleep. And what had made him say that to her? *I love you, Chelsea.* They hadn't spoken in nearly three years. She hadn't seen him since he'd been discharged from the Army.

His mother had invited her to his "Welcome Home" party, but Chelsea hadn't gone. How could she?

She couldn't imagine what he thought he needed to apologize about. After all, she'd been the one to break his heart. She'd been the one to get married while he was deployed.

Chelsea squeezed her eyes tightly to ward off any tears that might threaten. The Walkers had raised decent men, even the hot-tempered Russell. He hadn't deserved a two-timer like her.

The head nurse walked into the room. "Everything okay in here?"

"Yes. He woke up for a moment, but the pain meds kicked in."

The head nurse checked her watch. "Okay, you'll come back through in another hour and do this again. His surgery was major, and he'll need to be constantly monitored."

Chelsea nodded as she tucked her pen into her pocket and picked up her paperwork. She would certainly need to ask for a different rotation until he was better. Looking down at his bruised face and his cut up arms was breaking her heart. But she was sure that wasn't the deep-rooted source of her anguish.

His words were ringing in her ears. Any other day she'd have written them off as banter from a patient on meds. But this was Russell Walker—her first love.

Did he mean what he'd said? Because she'd never stopped loving him, even after she'd gotten married.

No wonder that hadn't lasted long.

Chelsea walked out of the room and down the hall to her next patient, but for the next hour, all she could think about was Russell Walker, and what might have been had she not have been so spiteful, and had waited for him to return home.

CHAPTER 2

*R*ussell watched the clock. He'd had three different nurses come in and take his vitals. Chelsea never returned.

He'd seen all of his brothers. His mother had sat in the chair knitting something most of the day, and his father had stopped in three times. Now he was alone. His dinner tray sat in front of him untouched, and his freaking leg hurt so much he thought he'd cry.

But the moment the door to his room opened, he perked up. Absolute disappointment filled his body as his cousin Jake walked through the door.

"Hey," Jake said as he closed the door behind him. "You've looked better."

"I feel like hell."

Jake removed his ball cap and ran his hand over his hair before replacing it. "Yeah, I've been there, remember?"

Russell did remember, though Jake had been much worse off. Not only had he crushed his leg and his arm, but he'd also had a life-threatening head injury to boot.

"What made you decide to race again after something like this? I can't even imagine driving again."

Jake grinned. "It's inside me. I have to go fast. Adrenaline junkie. Maybe when you're up and running, we'll hit the track, and you'll get over it."

Russell snorted a laugh, which hurt clear down to the toes he couldn't feel. "I think I'll be fine without it."

"I had Officer Smythe show me your truck. There's nothing I can do with it. But I'm having them bring it to my shop."

Russell sunk into his pillow. "Figured. I really messed it up, huh?"

"Dude, you're lucky to be alive," Jake said in a voice that could have been mistaken for his mother's. "You'd better just write it off and be grateful."

"Maybe I'll replace it with some little number like Gia's Mini Cooper."

Now Jake laughed, and Russell knew it was at the thought of the Mini-Cooper Gia owned. "I'd love to take that thing to the track."

When the door opened again, Russell looked to see which nurse would be coming his way with meds or needles, but to his surprise, Chelsea walked through the door, a duffle bag on her shoulder.

Their eyes locked, but they didn't say a word. She was obviously not coming to poke him.

"Hey, Chels," Jake was the first to speak.

Chelsea lifted her head, a look of surprise flashed across her face as if she hadn't even noticed there was someone else in the room.

"Hey, Jake. Sorry," she said shifting her attention back to Russell. "I didn't know you had company. I'll come back."

"Nope," Jake moved toward her, kissed her on the cheek, and pulled open the door. "I'll see myself out. Take care, cuz. I'll stop back by. You'll be here for a while."

The very thought made Russell's pain kick up a notch.

"Is he still racing?" Chelsea asked, gripping tightly to the strap of the bag that hung from her shoulder.

"Yeah. He didn't learn his lesson."

"I'm heading home. I just wanted to come back in and say that I'm glad you're okay."

"Come sit and talk. I really could use some non-Walker visit time."

Chelsea looked at her watch. "I only have a few minutes."

"I'll take them."

She bit down on her bottom lip and still gripped to the strap of the bag. "I probably shouldn't have come in. You need to rest and..."

"I wanted to see you," he said trying to adjust the slightest bit on the bed, but that only caused more pain. "It was a nice surprise to wake up to you this morning."

"I shouldn't have even started your vitals. I just didn't want to cause problems with my supervisor."

"You never came back."

"I traded floors. I thought it would be best."

"So you don't want to see me?"

She shifted the bag to her other shoulder and looked at her watch again. "Russ, I just want what's best for you. I'm not that. Not even now. I don't think me being your nurse would help you heal."

"Yeah. Having a gorgeous nurse might ruin my day," he felt the flame of his anger rise in his chest. "I'm surprised you bothered to stop on your way out. But I guess you're in a hurry."

"I am. I hope everything goes well for you. I know your family will be a great support for you."

"I'm sure they will," he reached for his bedside remote and turned on that damned TV he'd had enough of. "Guess I won't be seeing you again, huh?"

"It's better for everyone."

"Sure."

Chelsea looked at her watch one more time then stepped closer to the bed. "Russ, I wanted to apologize to you."

He turned off the TV. "You wanted to apologize to me?"

"Yeah. For back when we were together, and you were deployed. I'm sorry."

The memory of it came back to him. The moment he'd seen her that morning, none of that had come to mind. In fact, he was fairly sure he'd told her he wanted to apologize. Well, he sure as hell wasn't going to do it now.

Russell sat quietly. He didn't know what to say to that.

Chelsea moved closer to the side of his bed and leaned in to kiss him on the cheek. "You're in good hands. I have to go."

As she turned, he reached for her, which was a task, he'd realized as he pulled wires and tubes. "Please stop in again. I don't want us to leave things the way they were. I know you're married, and I know things didn't work out between us, but we were friends once. Remember?"

Chelsea took a breath, as if she had something to say, but instead, she continued to leave, closing the door behind her.

THAT HAD BEEN HARDER than she'd wanted it to be. Sincerely, Chelsea had gone to his room with the hope that they could find a common ground between them, but she couldn't do it. She couldn't even tell him she wasn't married anymore—or why she was in such a hurry.

Deep inside, she wanted to know what he had to apologize for and did he remember telling her he loved her?

Chelsea looked at her watch again. She was late now, and if she didn't get across town in a half hour, she'd be charged for being late. She couldn't afford that again. It sure would be nice to have a partner in life that could help with everything—or even family nearby. That was just one of the many things Chelsea regretted about her decisions. She could have been part of the Walker family, but no, she couldn't have been bothered to wait for the man she loved. She had made rash and stupid decisions.

She deserved what she got. She deserved Russell's anger.

Chelsea waited for the next elevator, counted the minutes as it stopped on each and every floor, and hurried through the lobby to the doors that lead to the parking lot.

Employees didn't have the luxury of curbside parking. No, she was going to have to sprint to get to her car and make it across town.

Yanking the door open, she threw her bag into the passenger seat and shut the door. Fumbling for her key, she finally managed it into the ignition and turned it. Nothing happened.

"No. No. No," she repeated to herself and tried again. Still, the engine didn't respond.

Chelsea threw her head back against the seat. The tears were there before she knew it. She couldn't afford late fees, and she couldn't afford car repairs. School payments were due soon, and if she didn't pay her cell phone by the end of the week, that would be turned off too.

The tears rolled down her cheeks now and everything inside of her broke. This wasn't how she'd planned her life, so why was it happening like this?

A knock at the window had her screaming. When she turned her head, she saw Officer Smythe backing up, his hands held in surrender.

Chelsea opened the door.

"Sorry, Chels. I saw you sitting here and wanted to make sure you were okay."

She wiped at her cheeks, brushing away the traces of tears. "My car is dead."

"I can give you a jump."

She tried to smile. "That would great. I'm late picking up Lucas."

"How about I give you a ride, and we can come back and fix your car."

The tears were back. "That would be fantastic." She wiped her cheeks again. "Forgive me. I'm a mess today," she said as she grabbed the bag. "Can you help me get his seat out of the back."

Phillip Smythe smiled with a nod. "Of course. He's getting big, huh?" He opened the back door and unbuckled the car seat.

"Yeah, he'll be three in a few months."

"Exciting age." Phillip pulled the seat out of the car. "I'm parked just over there," he said with a nod as Chelsea closed the door and locked the car.

"I really appreciate this."

"My pleasure. I was just headed in to see Russ. Did you know he was here?"

She bit down on her lip. "I talked to him. Of course, since I'm one of his caretakers, I guess I can't discuss it with you, even if we are friends."

He shifted a glance her way as they walked toward his truck. "You're one of his caretakers?"

"Student nurse rotation."

"How did that go over?" he asked as he unlocked his truck and opened the door for her.

"You're asking if he threw me out of the room?"

Phillip opened the back door and set the seat inside and strapped it in with the seatbelt. "Russ has a temper. I was with him when he found out you were married. That was a long night. I just…"

"He said he loved me before he passed out from the meds they have him on. So no, he didn't kick me out."

Phillip shut the door and walked around to the other side as she closed her door and buckled in. Phillip climbed in, and started the engine "I didn't mean to pry."

"Yes you did," she laughed, and he followed suit.

He put the truck into drive and started out of the parking lot. "He told you he loved you?"

"He's not fully there. They have him on a lot of meds to keep the pain down."

"His truck is totaled. He's lucky to be alive," Phillip's voice changed from humor to real terror. "He's an idiot. Not only did he get into a fricking fight at the bar, but he'd also been drinking."

"So he'll have a DUI?"

Phillip rubbed his forehead. "No. His blood work came back normal."

"So he was just going too fast?"

"You know what sucks? Both of our jobs have us tied to confidentiality. I shouldn't be talking about this."

"So there's more?"

He shot her a look. "Nothing leaves the confines of this truck?"

"Nothing," she promised.

"I think he was run off the road," he said, and Chelsea felt as though it had punched right into her gut.

"Someone did that to him?"

"I don't have my proof yet. I want to talk to him. Friend to friend. He'll tell me if he was drinking too much. There's medical proof that he wasn't, but were there other circumstances? I need to know what the fight was over. Maybe that'll help. No one at the bar said much."

Chelsea reached across the cab of the truck and touched Phillip's arm. "He looks horrible."

"I imagine."

She removed her hand and squeezed her arms around the duffle bag in her lap. "When I walked into his room I just stood there and stared at him. Both of his eyes are black. There are cuts all over his face and arms. His leg is bandaged from top to bottom. He broke his ankle, and they had to do surgery to remove debris that impaled him," she continued as her eyes welled with tears. "He's going to need a lot of physical therapy to get up and moving."

"He'll do it. And he'll do it far ahead of schedule too."

That made her chuckle. "He will."

"Did you tell him you're divorced?"

She turned to look at him. "No. Why would I?"

Phillip shrugged. "You said he told you he loved you."

The words hung there, just as they had when Russell had said them. "He's drugged up. Whatever he says can't be construed as truth. He did love me—once." And of course, she'd loved him since. The memory of him had forced her into many sleepless nights.

The reality of what she'd done to him always loomed. Though she wouldn't have Lucas if she hadn't strayed away from Russ. And though she'd rather have had Russ, and his temper, be Lucas's father, she couldn't deny that Lucas was her greatest gift in life. He far surpassed any silly love she'd had for Russell Walker. Lucas had kept her going in hard times. Sure, he was only nearly three-years-old, but he fed her soul.

Phillip pulled up in front of Martha's daycare. "I'll wait here for you."

Chelsea put her duffle bag on the floor. "Thank you for doing this for us. I'm sorry to take time out of your day."

Phillip smiled. "The only other thing on my agenda today is to talk to Russ. He's not going anywhere."

She chuckled and climbed from the truck. As she shut the door, she thought about Russ and his family. The Walkers and their five sons were tight knit. They had each other's backs, and as a team, they had the backs of relatives and friends. You were in good hands if you were associated with the Walkers.

She'd missed that part when she'd married someone else. The Walkers would still have her back. She knew that. But it would never be the same.

Chelsea opened the door to the daycare center and immediately saw her son following Martha around the table as he laughed. When he caught sight of her, he yelled, "Mama," and ran to her hugging his arms around her legs.

She might have missed out on a Walker last name, but the little man hugging her was worth more than that. How could she ever even consider that having waited for Russell would have been better than never having had this sweet little boy?

There was a time when she'd thought she'd known true love—when she was with Russell. But she hadn't found it until she held her baby for the first time. Sure, it was different than the love of a man, but it was absolutely pure. Perhaps that's where the universe meant for her to land. Not with Dominic and not with Russell. But she was meant to have that little boy.

CHAPTER 3

*D*rugs were supposed to be fun, Russell assumed, even though he'd never experimented with them. He'd thought they were supposed to give you a high better than alcohol.

He thought of the time he'd had his wisdom teeth out. He was loopy, and that was fun.

Clinging to a hospital bucket as he threw up the Jell-O he'd tried to consume, was not fun. Every time they touched his IV, it made him sick. They said anesthesia would do that to a person, although he was distinctly under the impression that when they gave you anesthesia, it was so you wouldn't feel anything. Why the hell did he still hurt so much, and why was he throwing up?

He lurched again just as the door to his room opened and Phillip Smythe walked in.

"Bad timing, man," he said as he laid back against his pillows.

"Food isn't that bad here," Phillip joked.

"I hate this. I freaking hate it," he said taking the wet rag the nurse had brought him and wiping his mouth. "The only good thing in my day was my nurse. Well, one of them."

Phillip smiled as he pulled a chair closer to the bed and sat down. "Chelsea?"

"How'd you know that?"

"I talked to her. Her car died. I jumped it."

Russell squeezed his eyes shut. "She knows how to do that. I taught her."

"Sure, but she was in a hurry," he said. "That's what friends are for, right?"

Russell set his bucket on the bed table and rested back. "She didn't seem to want to be friends with me," he admitted. "She transferred to another floor so that she didn't have to be in here."

"I don't think she knew what to do when you told her you loved her."

Russell winced. "I did say that, didn't I?"

"She said you did."

He looked at the IV bag to his side. "Truth serum pumped right into my veins, huh?"

Phillip laughed. "Could be." He rested his arms on his thighs and leaned in over them. "Speaking of that. I wanted to ask you a few questions."

"So you're not here just to visit as a friend."

"Of course, I am. But I want to get to the bottom of a few things."

"I wrecked my truck. Now I'm stuck in here. What else do you want to know?"

Phillip ran his hand over the back of his neck. "We've had a few reports that you got into a fight."

"I had some words with a guy. That's all."

Phillip nodded. "Words? He didn't attack you, or vice versa."

Russell sat up, only to quickly lay back again when the pain surged through him. "You're asking me if I hit the guy?"

"I'm asking you if anything happened."

"Just because some ass starts crap with me, you think I started a fight."

"No. I'm asking if you got into a fight."

Russell let out a long breath. "I didn't start anything. Some guy started in about my dad and comparing him to my uncle and his underhanded business dealings. That doesn't fly with me. My dad is an upstanding citizen. Just because his brother isn't, that shouldn't reflect on my family."

"That's all? Words over your dad?"

"He made some crappy comment about Chelsea too. I don't know who the guy was, but he knew she'd married someone else while I was deployed. I don't know why this crap has to surface three years later, but it did. I wanted to punch him, but I didn't."

Phillip scooted to the edge of his seat. "When you left, did he follow you?"

"I don't know that he followed me. I was just focused on getting out of there so that I didn't take the guy down."

He nodded and sat back as the door opened again and Lydia Morgan, a dear family friend, poked her head in.

"Hey, stranger. Interested in some..." she stopped as she noticed Phillip sitting there. "Oh, you have company. I'll come back."

She began to back out the door, and Phillip jumped up, hurried to the door, and pulled it open.

"He'd love your company," he said and looked back at Russell. "I'll talk to you later. If you think of anything else, let me know."

Russell nodded and watched as Lydia walked into the room and Phillip scanned a look over her. Did she know the man was obsessed with her? She didn't even acknowledge him.

Lydia turned her head as the door latched and let out a breath. "It must be a curse. That man is everywhere I go."

"He's embedded in this community as a police officer, just as you are with all the businesses you own," Russell defended.

"I suppose." She moved to his bedside and kissed his cheek. "How are you feeling?" she asked as she combed his hair back with her fingers.

"Like crap. I don't know what happened," he confessed. "I've driven that road for years. How did I run off the road and flip my truck?"

Lydia took his hand and held it. "I don't know, but maybe it'll come to you."

Russell looked at the woman next to him and wondered how she had managed to have such a kind heart when she'd been raised by her grandfather, who was a cold hearted man.

She straightened the blanket on his bed. "Was Officer Smythe questioning you? Doesn't he know you're recovering?"

"He was here to visit."

"Sure. His job rules his life. I'm sure he had ulterior motives to be here." She ruffled her short cap of hair. "I shouldn't say that. You're his friend and of course, he came to see you."

"Did you come to make sure I was alive?"

"Damn straight. I was counting on you to help me do some work on a new house I just bought."

Russell tried to turn his head to look at her but realized just how stiff his muscles had become. "You bought a new house? This is a business investment?" he asked, knowing that she had a weakness for buying up buildings in the town to run businesses out of. He knew she was well off with her grandfather's fortune alone, but he had a suspicion that she was doing just fine on her own as well.

"No, this is just for me," she said turning and taking the extra pillow off the dresser and walking to the other side of the bed. "It's a little cottage with a cute yard."

She gently lifted his arm which was bandaged from wrist to shoulder, and set it on the pillow. He felt the sudden relief he hadn't known he needed.

"You're moving out of your grandfather's?"

She smiled. "It's long overdue." Lydia adjusted her bracelet on her arm then turned her attention back to him. "I could still use some landscaping in the spring when you're all healed."

"I heard what they had to say. I'm lucky to be alive. I'm going to have to do physical therapy with all the work they had to do to my leg and hip."

"Consider working at my house therapy," she grinned and walked around to the other side of the bed again. "I should let you rest. You look tired."

Suddenly he felt it.

"Thanks for coming to visit."

She leaned in and kissed his cheek ever so gently. "I heard your brother is getting married."

That still stung. He'd had eyes for Gia Gallow, who owned a shop in one of Lydia's buildings, and his brother was now going to marry her. Maybe she'd seen right through him from the start. He was only trying to move on from his broken heart of three years. When someone promised to wait for you then married someone else, it hurt for a long time.

"They'll be good for each other," he said on a yawn.

Lydia gave his hand a gentle pat. "Get some rest. I'll stop by again."

THE LIGHT from the hallway streamed into Russell's room as Chelsea pushed open the door. He was sleeping, and she paused to watch him before entering.

Early morning rotations might have been her favorite if she weren't a single parent without support from her ex-husband or parents. Thank goodness she had dear friends who could stay with Lucas and take him to the daycare.

Chelsea walked into the room and signed into the computer. She took a moment to read the files about Russell's night, which hadn't seemed to have gone very well.

She noted his pain medication and his calls to the nurses' station.

He stirred next to her, and she watched as he fought to find comfort with minimal movement. The bruises on his face were darker now. Even then, he was as handsome as she'd remembered.

Russell's eyes fluttered open, and she took a step toward his bedside. "Good morning."

It took him a moment to focus on her. Many times, patients, even days after surgery, found themselves confused when they woke in a hospital room. She assumed, by his facial expressions, this was what he was going through.

Instinctively, Chelsea reached for his hand and held it. "You're still in the hospital. You're fine."

He blinked a few more times. "It's nice to wake up with you here," he said with a raspy voice.

Chelsea reached for his water and handed it to him. He took a sip, and she replaced it on the tray.

"Thank you," he said, gratefully.

"It looks like you had a long night."

"Days and nights run together here." He wiped his eyes with the hand which wasn't bandaged. "I just want to go home."

"Sooner than you think," she said as she moved back to the computer. "You'll heal better at home."

"Can you imagine how much fussing over I'll get from my mother?"

The statement had them both chuckling—sharing a moment.

"She'll be the best thing for you," she offered.

"I don't know. Waking up the past few days with you standing at my bedside has been nice."

Chelsea swallowed the lump in her throat and turned to pull the machine which would record his vitals closer to the bed.

He turned his head. "I thought you were transferring floors."

"What kind of nurse would I be if I left every patient that made me uncomfortable?"

He cringed. "I make you uncomfortable?"

She placed the clip that would read his oxygen saturation on his finger and pushed a few buttons so that the blood pressure cuff on his arm would inflate. Then she picked up the thermometer and scanned it across his forehead, noting the reading.

"Your vitals are looking good," she said retrieving the clip from his finger. "Can I get you anything?"

"A straight answer."

No, that certainly wasn't what she wanted to give him. "You should rest more. It's early."

"Time is all the same from my perspective. Do I make you uncomfortable?"

"No," she said softly as the door opened and another nurse walked in.

"Mr. Walker, you're looking well this morning."

"Yeah, feel like crap, though. When do I get to go home?"

The nurse laughed. "You've only had our hospitality a few days. You're ready to fly the coop?"

He shifted a glance to Chelsea and then back to the nurse. "Yeah. The view at home is better."

The nurse laughed, but the comment cut through Chelsea's heart.

She signed out of the computer as the nurse took his cup out into the hall to fill.

"Let me know if you need anything," Chelsea said, as it was part of her training.

"I'm fine."

"Today is my last day for this week. Then I'm off for three days." She felt the need to let him know he was safe from seeing her.

He nodded slightly. "I'm sure you'd rather be anywhere but here."

The thought of not looking in on him was breaking her heart. "I have some Christmas shopping to do. You know, Santa can only do so much on his own."

He snorted out a laugh. "You always did like wrapping gifts."

"I'm sure you'll be home before Christmas. I'll bet your mom will be happy to have you there."

"That or I'll ruin her Christmas cheer."

Chelsea moved to his bedside. "I don't think that could ever happen."

His eyes shifted to lock with hers. "It's been a long time since Christmas was wonderful."

Again, his words sliced through her, and it was all her fault. Christmas nearly three years ago was when she'd promised she'd be there when he returned—she promised she'd wait.

"This Christmas will be different," she offered, but she wasn't sure if she were assuring him or herself.

"Chels, I'm in a bad way, and I know it. My attitude more than even my wrecked body." He sucked in a breath. "You're stand-offish to me, and I don't blame you. I just want you to know it's been nice waking with you next to me. I know it's all that's left, but I appreciate it. You're going to make a fine nurse. I'm sure your husband is very proud of you."

Tears began to well in her eyes as the nurse walked in with his cup full of water. "Here ya go. I'll be back with pain meds soon. I want to see you get some food in you today. You can't live on Jell-O alone," she chuckled.

"I'll try," he promised.

Chelsea followed the nurse to the door and walked out as Russell turned on the TV. She deserved his hate and his bad attitude. She didn't deserve his appreciation and praise. At some point, she should tell him she failed at marriage. It would give him some pleasure, she was sure.

She rubbed her fingers between her eyebrows to ward off the headache that was starting.

"You doing okay?" the nurse asked, as she logged into the computer at the nurses' station.

"Yeah. Just a little headache starting. I'm getting used to these shifts."

The nurse laughed. "It gets easier. Wait until your night rotations start."

The very thought gave Chelsea a stirring of anxiety. Once she was done with her schooling, everything would be better. But for now, trying to juggle her schedule, and Lucas's was killing her. What she wouldn't give if her parents lived around the corner, like Russell's did.

Of course, had she been true to her heart, maybe things wouldn't be so tough. Glenda Walker could have been her mother-in-law and grandmother to her son. Had she waited for Russell, perhaps she'd still be married—to him—and not divorced from the ass she'd chosen over him.

Feeling sorry for herself did her no good. Besides, Lucas was the light of her life, no matter his paternity. She'd never give him up. At this point, she supposed, she only wished for things to be easier. Well, she'd brought that on herself. Now she was paying for it.

As long as Russell was laying in that bed, she'd take care of him. After all, he did say he loved her.

A smile formed on her lips, and the headache began to fade away. Even if it was a drug-induced statement, it still made her happy.

CHAPTER 4

*N*umerous noises were coming from his mother as the doctor put Russell's x-rays up on the light board in his room. She'd sighed, cried, sniffed, and he wasn't sure what else. His father's hand rested on her shoulder for comfort. Russell lay there, just as he had for nearly four days, waiting for them to say something positive.

"Everything is healing nicely. We're going to get PT in here today and get you moving a little bit. You won't be trying to walk for a few weeks, but you'll get there." The doctor took the x-rays off the board. "A few more days and we can release you into your parents' care. You will still need to be attended to at all times."

Russell realized that all the years of military training had led him to this moment. He wasn't about to let his mother wait on him hand and foot for the long term. He was physically in excellent health, minus this setback. He'd be damned if he wasn't going to be walking in a few weeks, just as the doctor had said— but fully walking, not assisted. No, Russell Walker wasn't going to rely on aids to help him get around.

"He'll be in good hands," his mother's shaky voice broke the silence Russell hadn't even noticed had filled the room. He'd been to locked into his own thoughts.

The door to his room opened again, and Phillip Smythe poked his head in as he took off his hat and secured it under his arm. "Oh, you have a full set of visitors. I'll check in later."

His mother rose and walked to the door, pulling Phillip inside. "You come in and visit. We've been here all morning. I could use some coffee," she offered, and Russell watched as his father fell into line next to her. "We'll be back shortly," she promised as they walked out of the room.

Russell looked at the doctor who was gathering his things. "I'll be back around tomorrow morning to check on you," he gave him a smile as he too walked out the door.

"Seriously, I feel as though no one wanted to see me," Phillip laughed as he walked around to the side of Russell's bed. "You look better."

"Get me the hell out of here, and I'll be even better. You passing through?" he asked as he looked at Phillip's uniform. "Or did you drop by on your coffee break?"

Phillip took his hat in his hands and ran his fingers over the rim. "There's surveillance footage of a blue pickup truck following you down the road. The gas station on the corner by the bar caught it on their camera."

Russell thought back to their first conversation. "You think I was run off the road, don't you?"

"I think there's a possibility. We're looking at your truck to see if we can find any other paint on it."

"My truck is blue, too."

"My team is good. They'll know if that was the case. Every blue is a little different."

"Jake said the truck is totaled. He can't fix it, and he can fix anything."

"He's right. You know you're lucky to be alive?"

"I've been told." He began to wish that sleep would just take over. Suddenly he didn't want to discuss the accident anymore.

"Dominic Cleary, does the name ring a bell?"

He wasn't sure if the beeps on the monitor grew more rapid because of the cuff on his arm or because of the name Phillip had just posed.

"Yeah, I know the name."

Phillip nodded. "I knew that."

"He's the S.O.B. Chelsea married." His jaw tightened uncomfortably, and his leg tensed so that the pain ripped through him. "Why the hell bring him up?"

Phillip rubbed his chin. "He's out on parole."

Russell fisted his right hand as anger surged through him. "Parole? He never hurt her, did he?"

Phillip rubbed the back of his neck. "He was in jail for robbery and kidnapping."

"That didn't answer my question"

"Russ, I'd better let you calm down before they kick me out of here."

"You'd better answer me, damn it," his voice rose.

Phillip took a deep breath. "He has a record of domestic violence. She has a restraining order against him."

Russell's vision began to blur. She didn't mention that, and he was pissed that she'd been in his presence for days without telling him. But then again, who'd want to brag that their husband was a felon?

"A restraining order? That means he's hurt her, and my guess is more than once. She's too trusting a person to have slapped that on him for just getting a little rough one time."

Phillip checked his watch. "I need to be getting back to..."

"You can't keep coming in here and dropping questions and walking out." He tried to sit up, and managed to move only slightly. "What the hell did he do to her to cause her to restrain him?"

Phillip bit down on his bottom lip. "He hit her when she told him she'd filed for divorce, and he took off with their son. They were missing for two days."

Russell eased back, and he fought the anger boiling inside of him mixed with the sheer sadness that struggled to surface in tears which stung at his eyes. "Son?"

"Lucas. He's nearly three."

The room grew warm, and suddenly Russell's world began to spin. The monitor to his side chirped loudly and within a few moments there were nurses piling urgently into his room. Phillip was pushed out as they readjusted Russell, fiddled with his wires, and added something to his IV. Then the world calmed, and went black again.

CHELSEA CHERISHED the days she could spend with Lucas. They'd watched TV together when he'd awoken at six in the morning. They'd shared a bowl of dry Cheerios for breakfast. Now, he rested in her arms as he napped, and she didn't have the heart to put him in his crib.

If these first three years had gone so quickly, she made herself sick thinking how quickly the next three would go. The overflowing sink full of dishes could wait until after he went to bed. She was simply going to hold him as long as she could.

With a glance at the kitchen table, which was filled with laundry and books, she realized she had homework that needed to be tended to as well. The very thought of it made her eyes burn, and she closed them hoping that Lucas's sleep would be contagious.

Just as she felt her muscles relax and her breath begin to sync to Lucas's, she heard a tapping at the door. Lucas remained quiet against her.

She rose carefully and walked him to the playpen where she set him down. He stirred briefly but found comfort quickly.

Chelsea hurried to the door and opened it to find Officer Smythe standing on her front porch. She pressed her finger to her lips and stepped outside, leaving the door open just a crack in case Lucas were to wake, so she would hear him.

"Lucas just fell asleep," she whispered as if to set the volume for their conversation.

"I'll be brief then," Phillip said, taking her lead.

"Is something wrong?" Her hands began to shake, so she fisted them behind her. "Is Russell okay?"

The corner of his mouth lifted in a grin. "You thought of him first?"

Chelsea pressed her shoulders back and crossed her arms in front of her. "You were working his accident. That's all."

He nodded, but she was sure he'd seen through that. "My reason for dropping by is different. Dominic was released from jail and is on parole in Texas."

Her lips began to tremble, and she pressed her hands to her stomach. "They should have warned me. They didn't warn me."

"I'm warning you." He reached for her and took her hands in his. "His parole is in Texas. He'll break it if he comes into Georgia."

"He'll come for Lucas."

"Do you really think he will? He doesn't want anything to do with him."

"He didn't want anything to do with him when he kidnapped him before either. All he wanted was to hurt me, and he did that."

"He's not going to come near you."

That was a truth she was much too familiar with. "I still have a restraining order, too."

"You do. All of this is intact. You need to know so that you're aware."

"Maybe I should go. I should move. My parents are in Florida with my sister. I could…"

He shook his head. "You need to stay here and finish school."

"I'm almost done. I'll take my boards, and then…"

"And then you'll heal the world." He smiled. "Until then, I think we need to make a plan to surround you with friends."

Chelsea swallowed hard. She hadn't had many friends in the past three years, only one or two she could count on to help with Lucas. Her breakup from Russell had cost her the friendships she'd had with his cousins and with his mother. Of course, that was her own fault. She'd pulled away from them altogether. Why wouldn't she? She was absolutely embarrassed.

They did still share some common friends. She was still close with Gia, but Gia wasn't expected to return home until after Christmas, though Dane had returned to check on Russell. And even when she did return home, she'd be much too busy planning her wedding to want to have Chelsea hanging around all the time.

There was Lydia. But Lydia was a busy woman. Chelsea had lost count of the number of businesses Lydia owned in town.

"I don't have any friends," she said.

"You have more than you think. But if you'll forgive me, I actually talked to someone else before I came over. Glenda Walker said they're going to need help with Russell when he comes home."

She felt the blood drain from her head. "That's not a good idea."

"Really? You have a better one?"

"Why would she do that? Why would she want to do that? And Russell probably thinks that's a horrible idea. I'd be better off living right here alone."

"You and Lucas alone? That's a solid idea," Phillip narrowed his gaze on her. "The Walkers are far enough out of town you wouldn't be followed around. There are enough of them, as well, to keep an eye on you and your son. Russell needs your expertise too. I don't see where this won't work out."

"I stabbed them all in the back, Phillip. I walked away from their family."

"Yeah, well Glenda must have forgotten, because this was her idea."

Chelsea walked to the porch step and sat down. Her knees had gone weak, and her stomach was unsettled. Phillip joined her, and they sat in silence for a moment.

"Do you think he'd really come here and hurt us?" She raised her eyes to his to read him even before he spoke.

"Chelsea, he took Lucas to hurt you. What says he won't do that again?"

"I never told Russell that I divorced Dominic. I never told him about Lucas."

He rubbed his chin and she could hear the scratching sound his whiskers made against his fingers. "I might have mentioned it to him."

She could feel the sting of the tears that would break free if she let them. "Icing on the cake, right? Broken promises because I strayed, got pregnant, and then married the bastard." Her stomach rolled, and she was sure she was going to be sick right there in front of Phillip, who was only there doing his job.

"We are all allowed our mistakes."

"But no one should hurt other people."

"It wasn't as if you were the one who ran him off the road."

She covered her mouth with her hand. "You think someone did that?"

"There is a small trail that leads to that." He rested his hand atop hers. "A lot of things can happen when people are apart like you and Russell have been. Sometimes the heart can forget the pain it had. Think about it. He did say he loved you." Chelsea dropped her shoulders and stared at him, but he only smiled back. "Russell needs you to heal him, and you need them to help you. Chelsea, think of Lucas. Don't think of the mistakes that led you here. Think about moving forward. The Walkers can help you do that."

Every sinner had to face their sins, she thought, as she later watched Phillip drive away. Perhaps her penance was in helping Russell heal at home while she was kept safe within the walls of his family's home.

While Lucas slept, she dug through the stack of mail on her counter that had grown over the past few weeks. Sure enough, there was the notice that her ex-husband was being released.

Her head had been in the clouds for months. Her lack of organization could have cost her and Lucas their lives had she not had someone like Officer Phillip Smythe looking after her.

Chelsea dug through her purse searching for her phone. She scrolled through the contacts until she came upon Glenda Walker's phone number. She needed to hear it from Glenda herself. She'd know in a moment if Phillip put her up to it or if it had been Glenda's idea—and she'd quickly know how Glenda felt about her. One thing Glenda Walker wasn't very good at was hiding her true feelings—no matter what they were.

$\mathscr{H}$ is father paced in front of yet another horrible daytime drama that played out on TV. His mother positioned a straw into another can of ginger ale, which he was beginning to despise as well. And Russell was captive to their fussing over him, which he'd decided wasn't the worst part of the hospital stay.

The muffled sound of his mother's phone came from within her purse. She stopped her fussing, dug in her purse, and pulled it out as she simultaneously greeted the caller.

A broad smile formed on her lips. "Chelsea, it's so nice to hear from you. I was just talking to Phillip about you earlier today. How is your son?"

Russell bit down on the straw his mother had just put into his drink. How had he missed this little part about her having a son, and why in the hell was she calling his mother?

"Well, I told him I thought it was best for everyone. Besides, it'll be great to have a little one around again." His mother moved to the window and looked outside, as his father walked to the side of his bed, and they both listened to the one side of the conversation.

"Yes, come out this evening. Susan is preparing something new for her catering menu, and she's bringing it over. I think you'll get along with her perfectly," she continued, and Russell gathered the sheet in his fingers and began to wad it into his fist as he listened to her. "We'll see you then."

She turned off the phone and slid it back into her purse before looking up and making eye contact with the two men who had been listening to her.

Glenda Walker went back to fussing over the lunch tray they had delivered to Russell, without another word. But his father stepped in, placing a hand over his mother's before Russell had a chance to question her.

"That was a cryptic call," he said getting her attention. "I think you should fill us in."

Her eyes were light and the dimples that deepened when she'd smile appeared. "It was nothing." She opened the napkin and set it on Russell's chest. "Okay, it was Chelsea."

Russell clucked his tongue. "You're having her over for dinner?"

"She's a very sweet girl, Russ. I've missed her coming around."

"So why now? What does she have to do with you?"

Glenda pulled the lid from the place and began to cut the meatloaf they'd sent up, which he certainly hadn't ordered. "Russ, she needs some help."

"Does this have to do with her husband being out on parole?"

"Ex-husband," she confirmed. "And yes. Phillip told me the story, and I said she and Lucas could stay with us. It would be a great comfort to have her there especially when you come home."

Russell pulled the napkin from his chest and threw it on the tray. "What are you doing? Chelsea and I are no longer a thing, Mom. What the hell makes you think that having her around is going to help me heal?"

His father pushed the tray out of the way. "Watch how you talk to your mother."

Russell let out a breath. "I'm sorry. This accident and having her around has messed with my head."

His mother stepped away from the bed and gathered her purse. "I think I should go. I have upset you, and that wasn't my intent, Russell."

"I know, Mom," he said with his voice softer. He reached for her with his right hand. She hesitated for only a beat before taking it. "Chelsea is a very special woman. I've never been able to let go of her," he admitted. "If you have grand ideas—this faith you have in pairing people—I don't know that it's a good idea. She hurt me, Mom. And today I found out she had a son and that the man she left me for hurt her. It's a lot to take in."

She patted his hand. "I know. But all of God's creatures deserve to have someone look after them. Including Chelsea and her son."

"She's very lucky to have you, and so am I."

The smile returned to his mother's lips. "Thank you. You get some rest." She kissed him on the cheek, picked up her purse, and headed out the door.

Russell and his father watched her walk away, but his father didn't leave.

"Dad, is something wrong?"

His father's brows drew together. "Phillip Smythe said something to me about thinking you'd been run off the road. What do you know about that?"

"Nothing, other than what he said. I don't remember being followed, Dad. But then I don't remember crashing either."

His father nodded and patted his hand just as his mother had, and then he left, leaving Russell alone again with only the monitor to his side making noise.

37

NERVES HAD NEARLY TAKEN over and stopped Chelsea from driving out to the Walker's house. She'd packed a bag for both herself and Lucas, just in case they stayed, though she wasn't sure of how the actual plan would play out.

Christmas lights hung from the gutters of the roof, and the thought that Glenda's house was already decorated for Christmas gave Chelsea a giddy warmth. The woman always was on the verge of going overboard with her decorations, but not quite. She couldn't wait to see it, and only hoped that Lucas could keep his hands off of things when they went inside.

Chelsea climbed from the car and opened the back door. Unbuckling his seat, he reached for her, and she pulled him to her. Kissing him on the cheek, she whispered to him, "I'll bet this is still the prettiest sight around at Christmas. This big ole house out here all by itself lit up like a Christmas tree."

When Glenda met them at the door, she'd enveloped them in a warm, loving embrace that had nearly brought tears to Chelsea's eyes. The woman acted as if three years hadn't passed, and as if Chelsea hadn't broken Glenda's son's heart as badly as she had.

Glenda reached out to Lucas, who to Chelsea's amazement, went right to her.

"Oh, you are a precious boy, aren't you?" she cooed and placed a kiss atop his little blond head when he rested it on Glenda's shoulder. "We're going to be good friends, you and me."

The nerves which had threatened Chelsea had now turned into a compelling mix of tearful emotion and regret. This could have been how things ended up had she waited. Had Chelsea not fallen victim to charm, Glenda would always have held her son that way, because he would have belonged to Russell.

"Are you okay, honey?" Glenda asked, and Chelsea realized that the tears that promised to rise, had.

"I'm fine. This is all a bit emotional for me." She gathered her thoughts. "Glenda, you're very kind even to have me in your home. I tore your family apart for a bit. I broke Russ's heart, and I can never take that back. I'm sorry."

Glenda pulled her in for another hug, this time, Lucas hugged her too. "People make mistakes," she said as she inched back. "But when I look in the eyes of this little boy I don't see a mistake. Much as when I look into the eyes of my step-son Eric, I only see a loved little boy who became a loving man. I didn't have to give birth to him to see it in him—but he's mine."

Her words squeezed at Chelsea's heart until she thought it might explode in her chest. "Thank you. I don't know how this is all going to work out. Russ might not want me around, but..."

Glenda smiled as she rubbed Lucas's back. "Oh, he does," she said, as she turned and walked toward the kitchen holding Chelsea's son in her arms.

The kitchen was just as she'd remembered it, only now a different woman, wearing an apron, hurried about from the island to the stove.

"Hi," she lifted her head from the pot she stirred. "I'm Susan. I'd shake your hand, but..."

"I understand. I'm Chelsea and that's my son Lucas," she said pointing toward Glenda.

Susan smiled. "Thank you for giving her a baby fix. She wants one of those, and Eric and I aren't quite ready yet."

Glenda swayed back and forth with Lucas, who had fallen asleep on her shoulder. "He's getting older, and you don't have much time," she sang as if she were singing a lullaby.

Susan laughed. "I'll tell him you said so." She continued to stir whatever was in the pot, which smelled divine. "So you're going to be staying here and helping when Russ gets home? I haven't seen him in a few days. Does he look any better?"

"He does look better. The bruises on his face are still pretty dark, but they'll go down soon. He'll do much better when he's here with everyone."

"And with you," Glenda whispered.

That still didn't sit well with her. She supposed they'd find out quickly enough. Russell would either allow her to help aid him back to health or kick her to the curb. Either emotion was valid and expected.

"Can I help here?" Chelsea asked Susan.

"I have it all under control. I'm a vegetarian, so everyone is gracious to try out my meat dishes. I'll be a little while yet, if you and Glenda want to go talk and make plans."

Glenda gave her a nod to join her in the other room.

Just as she'd imagined, the interior of the house was nearly drowning in elegant Christmas cheer. The Christmas tree was beautifully decorated and reached the ceiling. Christmas stockings hung over the mantle. Chelsea noticed that there were more than the usual seven Walker Christmas stockings. Now there was one with Susan's name and one with Gia's.

She looked away. Once upon a time there had been one that had her name on it too. They'd come that close, she and Russell. That stocking had probably been dropped into that very fireplace under the mantle, and burned with her memory.

"I brought a blanket to set on the floor for him. You don't have to keep carrying him while he sleeps," she offered to Glenda.

"You have no idea how much this does for my heart. It's been a very long time since my boys were this size. I never had the chance to snuggle Eric like this. He was eight by the time I became his mother. But I made sure I snuggled the other four until they could run from me."

"I can't imagine any of them would ever have run from you," she said with a laugh as she sat down next to Glenda on the sofa.

"Russell and Dane were the ones who didn't take to my excessive affection. Always wanted to do things on their own. Now, Ben and Gerald, they were my love bugs." She smiled warmly. "It's a healing kind of feeling, don't you think? When you can just sit, and hold your child?"

That was exactly what it was, Chelsea thought, and she'd used it as such, many times over the past three years.

Glenda adjusted on the sofa so that she could better look at Chelsea, but she never set Lucas down. "I know you're uncomfortable being here. I don't want you to be."

Chelsea wasn't sure what to say to that, and Glenda didn't offer her a chance.

Glenda rubbed Lucas's back. "I don't know what happened between you and Russ that ended things. It's not my business. You married someone and had this beautiful baby. That's in the past. Phillip Smythe has filled me in on your ex-husband, so I know a little about what you've gone through." She pressed a kiss to Lucas's head as he stirred slightly. "He seems to think there's a need to keep you around people and that's what I expect to do. You've been a vital fixture to this family in years past, and I don't want to see anything happen to you or your son. My son needs your skills and I think your company would offer him a lot of comfort."

"Mrs. Walker," she finally interrupted. "Your invitation means more than I could tell you. I'm grateful for everything. I want to tell you that things will be okay, and I don't need to be hidden away, but I can't say it with conviction. And knowing that my ex-husband has kidnapped my son once, I can't assure he wouldn't do something like that again. But I don't want to put any of you in danger."

"You won't be. Trust me. Nothing will happen to you or anyone in this family."

Chelsea eased a bit. "Thank you. But when it comes to Russell, I don't know where he stands on me being here. He needs to heal and he needs therapy. I might hinder that."

"I think you're the right medicine for it." Glenda rubbed Lucas's back again. "Don't you worry about Russ. You let me worry about him."

"Thank you."

"Now, we have made room for both of you upstairs. I think, for now, you should stay away from your house and keep Lucas out of daycare."

"But I have school and training."

Glenda nodded. "Lucas will be fine here with us. We will pay you to take care of Russell. And I have already been in touch with your school, and under supervision, they will approve you to work with Russell since your emphasis is on home health care and therapy anyway. It's as if it were meant to be."

Chelsea sat across from Glenda Walker, her mouth open, dumbfounded. She wasn't sure if she was supposed to be enthusiastic about the opportunity or mortified that she had done such a thing.

"I...I don't know what to say."

Glenda scanned a look over her. "You don't know if you should be thankful or upset."

Now how did she know that? "Mrs. Walker..."

"Glenda."

Chelsea took a breath. "Glenda, I don't know what to think or what to say."

"You don't say a word," she patted her hand. "I know that this isn't what you planned, and I suspect that spending time with Russ isn't something you're looking forward to either."

Chelsea wanted to say something, but she wasn't sure what. A paying job where she was comfortable, that was an absolute bonus. And the way she understood it, Lucas would be with her, or around her, at all times.

Then it hit her and she even gasped. Russell had said he loved her the other day. Should that matter? Did he mean it? Did he now regret it?

"I'm afraid that my being here will cause everyone discomfort."

"I believe that everything happens for a reason, no matter what it is." She winked. "Chelsea, perhaps fate didn't have you

42

marrying my Russ. Maybe it was fated that you came back into his life in this capacity only, but I don't believe that."

Lucas lifted his head and looked at Glenda. Chelsea waited for him to fuss, but he didn't. He looked around and when he saw her there, he reached for her, and she pulled him to her. Was that a sign? Any other stranger, he would have screamed, but not with Glenda.

There had to be an apology to her, one that encompassed her regret to the entire Walker family, before she accepted the offer—because she wasn't stupid enough not to consider it.

"Before I make my decision, I need to say something," she said as she turned Lucas to sit on her knee. "I can't even explain what possessed me to do what I did." She gave Lucas a squeeze. "It was disrespectful to your entire family."

"You can't look into his eyes and think that."

Chelsea pressed her cheek to his head. "He is my entire world. But I hurt Russell. I hurt all of you."

"We all rebound. Russell included. Please come live with us, work for us, and get Russ back on his feet."

It was the generosity and sincerity of Glenda Walker that had Chelsea seriously considering the offer.

"I would be honored to do this for you all."

The smile on Glenda's lips widened. "That makes me very happy. I'm very excited to have you both here," she said taking Lucas's hand and he giggled.

"But I want to talk to Russ first," Chelsea said. "I want to be the one to tell him that I'll be here."

Glenda's smile faded, only slightly. "If you think that would be best."

"I do."

She nodded, but Chelsea wasn't sure she agreed. It wasn't something she could worry about. It was the right thing to do, and God knew she'd done enough wrong by Russell. It was time she did something right.

CHAPTER 6

 or the first time, in a very long while, Chelsea felt at
 ease as she drove toward town. Sure, Martha took
great care of Lucas, but that morning when she'd left him in the
arms of Glenda, he'd smiled and waved goodbye. He knew he was
in good hands, too.

It felt odd to be going to the hospital when she didn't have a
shift. That could be the fact that her heart was ramming in her
chest, her palms were damp, and her stomach clenched at the
very thought at what Russell might have to say about his mother's plan.

Chelsea parked in the visitor lot and walked into the hospital.

Deciding that she needed a few more moments to calm
herself before going up to talk to Russell, she stopped in the
coffee shop and ordered a coffee. As she waited, she noticed the
chocolate chunk cookie in the case. Knowing Russell's dietary
restrictions had been lifted, she thought it might ease her
entrance if she walked in with his favorite cookie.

Moments later she walked down the hall to his room.
Standing just outside his door, she took a minute to collect
herself before pushing open the door.

The room was dark, and Russell lay peacefully asleep. She could turn around, and he'd never know she was there, but that wasn't the purpose. This time, she was there for him. She'd wait for him to wake.

Chelsea set her purse in the chair by his bedside and the bag from the coffee shop on his table. She shrugged out of her coat and draped it over the back of the chair.

Taking her coffee, she walked toward the window and gazed out over the city she loved. She could have gone to Florida with her family, but she knew she would never have been happy. It was hard staying in Georgia, and making it all work with a baby and school. But she was doing it, and they were doing okay. Well, that was until the news that Dominic was let out on parole.

She blew through the lid of her coffee absentmindedly to cool her drink.

It would all be okay, and she'd have those around her to thank for that. Between Phillip Smythe and the Walker family, she and Lucas would be just fine. But she couldn't help but worry a little. Dominic had kidnapped Lucas once before. He'd been driven to do it by his mother, when Chelsea had said she'd wanted full custody. It had been the longest and worst two days of her life. She couldn't imagine what he might do if he came back to Georgia now. And what if his mother still held a grudge against her for making sure the law kept them all away from her? How long could his parole hold him to Texas?

Her hands began to shake again, and panic rose in her chest.

Maybe now was the perfect time for her to leave Georgia. He'd come for her if he could, and not because he wanted her or Lucas. He'd come to hurt them.

RUSSELL OPENED HIS EYES SLOWLY. The day would come, soon, when he opened his eyes and the room would be his room.

He took a quick inventory of everything strapped to him

before he tried to adjust for comfort. He knew he'd go home with his arm bandaged. Of course, he'd have that stupid bandage on his leg for weeks to come. At least he'd walk again, though he'd been told that would take some therapy. It'd be nice if he could walk out of that freaking hospital on his own two feet, but now he'd just like to get out.

Movement at the window caught his attention, and he turned to see a woman standing in the shadows. Her back was turned to him.

It wasn't just any woman. It was Chelsea.

No matter how nasty they'd been to each other since he'd been there, something in his heart lightened when he saw her.

"Chelsea?" His voice was raspy and soft as it broke the silence of the room causing her to flinch and splash herself with the hot liquid in the cup.

She jumped back and wiped at her shirt. Then she looked at him.

"Hi," she said setting her cup on the table.

"Which arm do you want to poke on?" he asked as he blinked heavily, realizing he hadn't yet shaken his sleep completely.

"I'm here to visit. I'm not your nurse today."

That got his attention as he shifted in the bed to look at her. "You're here to visit? Another one of those 'I'll get another shift' kind of visits?" The thought stung, and he realized it had quickly taken a slice at his mood.

"No. I need to talk to you, so I'm here to visit."

He studied her in the dim light. "Open the blinds. What time is it?"

"Nine," she said walking to the window, opening the blinds, and walking back to him.

"Nine? Damn. Whatever they give me knocks my ass out."

"It's meant to. You heal better if you're rested and not in pain."

At the moment, looking at her, the pain wasn't in his limbs. It was in his heart.

BERNADETTE MARIE

"You have a son," he said, and Chelsea sucked in a breath and held it before she spoke.

"Lucas. He's almost three."

"Does he have your father's name as his middle name?"

He noticed her wince. They'd discussed that when they'd once planned a family.

Batting her eyes against the tears he'd seen well up, she nodded. "Yes."

Russell raised his bed to sit up, and Chelsea adjusted the pillows around him. She might not be attending to him today, but it was in her to always comfort people, that much hadn't changed. "Thank you," he said. "Smythe told me your ex-husband is on parole in Texas."

She bit down on her bottom lip. "Yes."

"He hurt you." His is voice was a curt whisper.

"He did. He wasn't the man I thought he was. I made a mistake."

"Doesn't mean he should hurt you," he offered shaking his head.

She batted her eyes. "He kidnapped Lucas." The first tear fell, and she quickly wiped it away. "He had him for two days before they found them in Texas. He'd abandoned him in the back of a car and robbed a liquor store."

"That's what sent him to jail?"

She nodded. "Yes. They added the charges for domestic violence."

"Violence?" Russell's voice grew sharp.

"Like I said, I made a mistake."

Russell reached for her hand and held it in his. "No, he did."

"I just wanted to tell you how sorry I was for everything I put you through." She wiped at the tears that rolled down her cheeks. "I've wanted to say I'm sorry for so long, but I was embarrassed. I've lived this close to you for all these years and…"

48

"Shh," he hushed her. He hated when she cried. "Water under the bridge."

"Are you kidding me?" Chelsea's voice cracked under her tears. "I can't even tell you why I did it. I loved you so much, and I was so excited that you were coming home. We had so many plans, Russell. So why...what makes someone...I mean..."

"Chelsea, stop." He squeezed her hand. "I've never been so hurt in my life."

"That doesn't help."

"I'm just being honest." He gave her hand a tug. "Get a chair and sit down with me. I'm getting a pain in my neck looking up at you." He smiled, and she let out a quick laugh.

Chelsea pulled the chair up to the side of his bed and sat down. "I brought you a cookie from the coffee shop and a little carton of milk."

He knew the grin on his lips had to match the lightness in his heart at the moment. "You know me pretty well, don't you?"

"Well, I did," she said reluctantly.

Russ pulled the bag to him with his free hand.

"Let me help you," she offered.

Chelsea took the bag and pulled out the napkin. She laid the cookie on it and then took out the milk.

"Do you want it open to sip it or dunk?"

"Oh, dunk."

Chelsea laughed as she opened the full top of the carton and set it on the table. She then pushed the table closer to him so that he could reach it with his good arm.

Russell picked up the cookie, broke it in half, and dunked one of the halves in the milk. When it was just right, he pulled it back and took a bite.

"That's the best thing I've had in a week," he moaned as he chewed. "Thanks."

"It was the least I could do. I wasn't sure how this visit was going to go down."

"Because you came to tell me that you're going to be my nurse when I get home?"

Chelsea sat back down and clasped her hands in her lap. "So you already know about that?"

"No. All I know is my mom is excited to have you at the house with your son. And she thinks it would be a good thing to have you there when I get home. I can only imagine that's so you can take care of me."

"And what do you think of that?"

He pushed the table away and took a deep breath. He'd had all night to think about it.

"I don't think it's a good thing at all." He cleared his throat. "I've been so mad at you for the past three years. I mourned us. I was pissed as hell. Confused. Then I wake up in the hospital, and you're here. Suddenly...I don't know what to think."

"So, I should let your mom know this isn't going to work." She stood and pushed back the chair. "I'm going to go pick up Lucas and..."

"Sit down," he ordered, and he noticed how gruff it sounded.

Chelsea stood there frozen. He kept his eyes locked on hers then looked back at the chair as if to direct her back to it.

Slowly she sat back down, twisted her fingers together, and kept her eyes to the floor.

"Russ, there's no reason for me to stay if you think this is all a bad idea."

"Look at me," he demanded quietly. Chelsea lifted her eyes. "You're leaving me hurt. I didn't know about Lucas until yesterday."

"That's why I was in such a hurry the other day. I had to pick him up."

"I just wish I'd known." He reached for her again. "My mom wants to protect you and Lucas. She thinks that having you around our family will do that."

"I know. I'm very thankful for her generosity."

"Chelsea, I'm so mad that you were involved with a man that would hurt you."

"I know. I think about it every day."

"I never would have done that to you."

Chelsea bit down on her lip. "I know. I hate myself for what I've done to you—to me."

"Don't say that. I suppose the part of my mother inside of me knows that it was fate. We weren't meant to be together, but I guess it doesn't mean we can't be friends."

She sniffed back the tears. "Friends is a good start," she said as she sniffed. "I don't know that I deserve your friendship, but I'd like to be your friend."

"Good," he said rubbing his thumb over her knuckles. "So you're going to be living in the house? Both of you?"

"Yes. Your mother has arranged for me to finish my training, supervised, while helping you recover."

His smile widened. "I think you're exactly the medicine I need."

"Russ, I'm so sorry."

"You have to stop saying that." Her apologies were making him nearly as mad as the act of losing her. "And I have to stop being mad," he said, realizing it was a two-way street. He rested his head back against the pillow. "I told you I loved you the other day, didn't I?"

Chelsea wiped away the rest of her tears. "You did. You were heavily sedated."

Russell nodded. "I guess that means it came out of sincerity, right? Truth serum?"

She laughed. "I suppose. You also said you wanted to apologize to me, though I can't imagine why."

He turned his head to look at her. "I wanted to apologize for being wrong for you. Somewhere I must have done something that drove you to love someone else. I'm sorry for whatever that was."

Chelsea pulled her hand from his and stood with her back turned. He could see her shoulders rise and fall. She was crying. Perhaps he'd done something horrible to drive her away, though he didn't know what that was.

"Chels…"

"I was afraid you were going to die in combat, Russ. I had it in my head that you wouldn't come back to me. I got angry about it, and I pushed myself away from your family." She turned back frantically wiping at her tears. "It's stupid. I get that. But I'd met a few girls who had husbands and boyfriends who were deployed, and they felt the same way. One of them told me her fiancé had cheated on her with a woman who was stationed with him. It made me worry. Then the other woman said she'd started drinking because she worried about her husband so much. When I thought about it, all I could think about was how much we would fight. You and I were always at each other, so how were we going to be fine when you got home?"

She covered her mouth and walked back to the side of his bed. "It's stupid. It's all so stupid. I worked myself up so much over it that lost all common sense. Then my family moved away, and I was alone." She sucked in a breath. "I knew Dominic for a week before I let him take me home. I thought maybe that's what I needed. I needed someone who was here for me."

Russell squeezed his eyes shut. He wasn't sure he wanted to hear this, but he knew she needed to say it.

He opened his eyes and looked at her urging her to continue with a nod.

"Russ, you never did anything to push me away. I let my mind do that, and it did a good job. I was wrong." She moved to her purse and pulled out her phone. "I got pregnant three months before you returned. In fact, the day I got your message that you'd be coming home was the day I found out."

She sat back down in the chair and scrolled through her phone. "I had decided to admit that I'd had an affair and face the consequences. I didn't plan to get pregnant. Dominic and I got married a week later."

Chelsea lifted the phone so that he could see the screen. "This is Lucas."

Russell looked at the little boy in the picture, and his chest tightened, and it pained him to look at him. He had her blond hair and blue eyes. The smile on his face was contagious, and he knew he'd begun to smile just looking at him.

"He's a beautiful little boy," he said, and she looked down at the picture and smiled.

"He's amazing, Russ. He's my entire world."

"As he should be. Chelsea, I'm okay with you being at the house when I get home. I don't know that I'll be a very good patient, but…"

She laughed. "You'll be horrible, but I'll take that as payment for what I've done."

Russell shook his head. "You've already paid enough. It's time to forgive yourself. You have Lucas. He should be your priority. I'm just your job now."

"You could never be just that."

Their eyes lingered on one another, and he knew that he had spoken the truth that first day. He did still love her.

She leaned in and pressed a lingering kiss to his cheek. "Thank you," she said as the door opened and she quickly stepped back from him.

The nurse walked in and began her charting of his vitals. It was obvious to him that the women didn't know each other.

Chelsea picked up her purse and her coat. "I'm going to head out. Phillip said he'd meet me at my house so I could collect a few things."

That told Russell that things were a little more serious than anyone had let on. They were worried enough to have her leave her house and not go back without an escort.

"Are you working tomorrow?"

She shook her head. "I'm only in-house for now. It's better that way."

"Right. You'd better get back before my mom spoils your son."

She laughed. "He could use some of it. He loves her," she said, and her eyes lit up.

"What's not to like? My mother is magic."

Chelsea nodded as she walked out of the room and Russell rested back.

Yeah, his mother was magic. Who'd have thought she'd somehow manage her magic between him and Chelsea.

He closed his eyes, let the nurse finish her job, and he thought of Chelsea and her son. Somehow he'd gone from despising the woman to being her friend again. But nothing had hurt as much as seeing her son's face. That might just be a betrayal his heart couldn't overcome. They could be friends because he believed she truly needed one. But that feeling of love that kept creeping into his heart—that needed to go. He never wanted to be hurt like that again.

CHAPTER 7

*T*he music on the radio seemed a little cheerier, and the holiday decorations that hung on the lamp poles brought happiness to Chelsea.

The very thought of being surrounded by the Walkers for Christmas made her smile, alone in the car.

When she pulled up in front of her house, Phillip Smythe was already parked there. As she parked behind him, he climbed from his patrol car and walked back to her.

He looked in the backseat as she slipped out from the car.

"Where's Lucas?" His voice tremored with worry.

"Glenda Walker has him."

Phillip eased. "Good. He's safe there."

"You seem concerned."

Phillip took off his hat and ran his hand over his hair, which always was a sign he was upset about something. "I haven't talked to Russ yet, but they found evidence of the other blue pickup's paint on his truck. He was pushed off the road."

Chelsea stepped up to him and placed her hand on his arm. "That's horrible. Why would someone do that? I know he runs his mouth but..."

"The pickup we tracked down belongs to Dominic."

She felt the blood drain from her head, and she leaned against the car for support. "He wasn't out when Russell got in his accident."

"You're right. And we've confirmed that he's still in Texas. A deputy even went out and saw him at his residence."

"I don't understand," she pleaded as she eased from her position against the car. "Why would someone do that? Why would they use Dominic's truck?"

"I'm looking into that. But, Chels, if they were willing to hurt Russ that badly, and he hadn't even been in contact with you, it worries me now that you have been with him."

"You think Russell is in some trouble?"

Phillip shrugged. "He's not a troublemaker. Sure, he has a short fuse, but he's not a problem. There has to be more to it. We're trying to find who was driving the truck that night."

"How did you know it belonged to Dominic and not know who was driving it?"

Phillip pointed across the street to where a blue pickup truck sat parked at the curb. "We found the truck two hours ago, right there."

Her head began to spin, and she must have swayed because Phillip's arms came around her. "Let's get you inside and get you some water."

"You're sure Dominic is still in Texas?"

"I'm sure," he assured her as he helped her into the house.

THE NEWS HAD FINALLY COME in. They would plan to send Russell home in two more days. He wasn't sure he could make it two more days. All he wanted was the comfort of his own bed.

When the door opened to his room, he couldn't help but hope it might be Chelsea, but then he quickly reeled that thought back in. No, he'd have plenty of time with her. It wasn't going to do him any good to be hoping for her, if he was going to try and keep his heart at a distance.

So when his cousin Jake rounded the door, he was pleased to see him.

"Oh, you look a lot better," Jake said as he pushed the door closed.

"Yeah, I feel better. They said two more days, and they'll send me home."

"Good for you. Damn, I was in traction for weeks."

"Yeah, well, I wasn't going two hundred miles an hour."

Jake laughed as he pulled the chair up next to the bed and sat down. "It took me a year to walk. It looks like you'll be up and running soon."

"I'd like that," Russell said as he adjusted the sling on his left arm.

"So...Chelsea?" His cousin grinned. "What's that story?"

"She's my nurse."

"No kidding?" He laughed as he leaned his forearms on his knees. "You land in the hospital, and your ex is your nurse. Do they do regular checks on that IV to make sure she doesn't add anything to it?" He sat back in the chair as he laughed. "Damn, if that were one of my ladies, they'd have poisoned me for sure."

"Probably, but Chelsea isn't like that."

"So what's going on there? I haven't heard you talk about her without snarling in years."

Russell wanted to be snide and mad. He did that well and had for years. Jake had been one of his partners in drinking Chelsea's memory away more than once.

But he didn't feel that way right now. "She's moving in with my parents. Her and her son."

Jake raised his eyebrow. "Dude, that's weird."

"Well, my mom has a soft heart. She wants to protect her from

57

that ass she married. He was in prison. I guess she's divorced, and they have a son."

"Serves her right for what she did to you," he said crossing his arms in front of him. "Women are trouble, especially those that cheat on you."

Russell picked up his water and took a sip. He and Jake had had these conversations, but to hear him talk about Chelsea that way hurt.

"People make mistakes. She made hers. She cheated, got pregnant, got married, then…" He stopped and coughed, literally choking on his words. "Then, from what I gather, he must have abused her. Somewhere between that, and her getting a divorce, the S.O.B. kidnapped their kid, drove to Texas with him, and abandoned him in a car while he unsuccessfully tried to rob a liquor store."

"Shit," Jake sighed.

"Yeah. Well, now he's out on parole. There seems to be some concern that he'll jump parole and leave Texas to come here. So now my mom is involved, and Chelsea and her son are staying with my parents."

"Aren't you going home when you leave here?"

Russell nodded. "Yep. Home, and she's now my nurse."

"This is messed up, man. What are you going to do with her there? You never did get over her."

So, it had been that obvious. "I won't go through that again, but I can be her friend. She needs one."

Jake grinned as he ran his tongue over his teeth. "I wouldn't want to be in your shoes," he said as he stood. "I have to get back to work. I have one more car to get out of the garage by five. I'm glad you're doing better."

"Thanks," Russell said as Jake waved and headed out of the room.

Russell welcomed the quiet. He hadn't realized how much he'd tried to forget Chelsea until Jake had come in. He had cursed her name too many times, as Jake had pointed out. He hadn't been raised like that. She must have really gotten under his skin.

Sure, he'd dated since then, but it had never been the same. All along it was supposed to have been Russell and Chelsea. When that didn't happen, then nothing was that important.

Russell turned on the damned TV again. Was it fate that Ross and Rachel were on talking about being on a break? He chuckled to himself. Was that what Chelsea had thought when she fell in love with Dominic? He didn't know the man, no more than knowing his name. What could have possibly lured her into his arms?

It didn't matter now he thought as he turned the channel to the Food Network. Chelsea had her issues, and he had his own. She had a son to raise and schooling to finish. He was going to be getting back on his feet.

Even having her living in his house wasn't going to change what had happened between them. In time, his mother would see that. They'd either be amicable or go separate ways.

As Guy Fieri drove off in his fancy red car on the TV, Russell turned it off. Knowing that Dominic had hurt her wasn't sitting well with him. No one should have ever hurt her, not matter what. So, she'd decided not to love him anymore, fine. But why chose someone that would hurt her and kidnap their son?

The need to protect her rose in his mind. They might not be lovers anymore, but he felt the need to make sure she and Lucas were safe forever.

He smiled to himself. Perhaps that part of his mother's grace lived inside of him after all.

Suddenly, he wanted her at his house helping him recover. Maybe that would help them all. And he knew, without a doubt, his mother was going to have the time of her life having a little one around the house. She'd been hounding Eric and Susan for a grandbaby since they'd gotten married. He assumed Gia and Dane would be feeling that wrath too, soon.

Maybe he'd send one of his brothers out on a quest to buy Lucas a Christmas gift from him since he wouldn't be wandering the malls anytime soon.

He rested his head back against his pillow. In his mind, he had found some peace with having Chelsea around. With any luck, there would be the same peace when they were living under the same roof.

CHAPTER 8

*P*hillip guided Chelsea toward the house with his hand on her back. She was very aware that he had his eyes scanning in every direction as she unlocked the front door and pushed it open.

As soon as they stepped inside, and she closed the door, he held up his hand.

"Stay here," he whispered as he walked further into the house.

Chelsea, out of instinct, laced the keys on her ring through her fingers like a weapon and held tightly to the doorknob.

She watched as Phillip maneuvered through the house as if he were checking for something. A few moments later, he returned.

"I don't see that anyone has been in here. The back door is still locked. The windows are closed. Nothing seems disrupted. I want you to look around and make sure."

Chelsea nodded as she let go of the door and walked through the house, the keys still tucked between her fingers.

Each room looked the same as she'd left it the day before. Even the sink still had dishes that needed to be tended to. Perhaps Phillip would understand that she needed to take care of that before they left the house.

"Once we leave here, I don't want you coming back here, understood? Pack what you need to stay at the Walkers' and stay clear."

She nodded. "Do you think someone has been watching me?"

"Chels, none of this makes sense. But it's my job to get to the bottom of it. Someone ran Russell off the road with a truck belonging to your ex-husband. That same someone parked that truck across the street from your house, but your ex-husband is still in Texas. Not a lot adds up right now. As soon as we're done here, and I know that you're safe at the Walkers', I'll reach out to the department in Texas to have them interview your ex-husband."

"I hope he cooperates. Nothing can happen to Lucas. Promise me that nothing will."

"Trust me, as a friend. I would never let anything happen to him, or you, again."

Chelsea had done the dishes in the sink and packed more clothes for herself and Lucas.

Luckily, this time, she'd remembered the Tigger, which had fallen behind the bed. That should help Lucas ease into life at the Walker's house. Toiletries were gathered and even some of the food she'd spent her budget on, she took with them.

As she unpacked her clothes and put them in the dresser drawers at the Walkers', she thought of how ironic it was that she was now living in Russell's old bedroom. She'd only been in there a few times, but they'd made plans once to live in that very room. Oh, they'd been young and stupid, she could say that now. They'd planned a whole life where they lived on the ranch in the very house in which he'd grown up. How interesting they hadn't thought of starting their own lives away from the land his family owned. Russell's mind had always been set on living there and working the ranch with Eric.

Lucas sat on the bed watching a movie on her iPad as she made the room look like home to them. A knock at the door had her stopping as Glenda pushed open the door slowly.

"How's it coming along?"

Chelsea pushed in the dresser drawer. "It's going well. You have no idea how grateful I am to be here."

"Phillip told me about the truck. I'm glad you're here too. I just thought I'd let you know that they're going to let Russ out in two days."

Her heart jumped in her chest. "That's fantastic."

"I'll be happy to have him home," Glenda pressed her hand to her chest. "Dane said Gia called, and she will be back here before Christmas too. Her plans have changed. I'll have my entire family here."

As happy as she was to be there, Chelsea felt the pang of guilt tug at her. She would be part of that family now, but she didn't belong. "My parents aren't able to come out until the end of January. I'm very thankful that we will be here with you all. I hope we won't be in the way."

Glenda moved to Chelsea and placed her hands on her arms. "You are part of our family. Family doesn't have to be blood."

"I'm honored to have you think of us in that way. I don't deserve your compassion."

"Never think that." She kissed her on the cheek. She looked at Lucas sitting quietly on the bed. "You know Santa hasn't been to my house in years. I think we'd better make some cookies for him," she said to Lucas. "What do you think? Would you like to do that with me?"

His eyes widened, and he jumped from the bed and ran straight to Glenda, taking her hand.

"You get settled in. Lucas and I are going to go make a mess of the kitchen," she said with a laugh.

Chelsea watched as Glenda Walker walked away hand in hand

with her son. It was a sight she'd dreamed about for years. Who knew it would happen?

What would Russell think if he'd seen them? Would it make him mad?

She supposed they'd find out in two days. Then Christmas was only a few days later.

Phillip had the gifts she'd bought for Lucas with him so that he wouldn't see them. They weren't many, and now she wished she had something for Glenda and her family. Maybe she could convince someone to take her to town. She certainly didn't want to go alone.

There was another knock at the door and this time, Gerald was standing there with a bouquet of daisies. "Mom thought you'd like these to brighten your room."

She could feel the tears form, but she pushed them back. "That is very sweet of her," she said as she took them and set them on the dresser. "I hope I'm not putting everyone out by being here."

"Of course not. She's giddy to have you here and your son. They are in the kitchen laughing and having a great time."

"I'm glad. With my parents living in Florida now, he doesn't get to be with them. And of course Dominic's family...well, they're not allowed to have anything to do with him after Dominic kidnapped him."

"He's safe now, and so are you," Gerald said, sitting down on the bed. "I have the room downstairs, off the kitchen, ready for Russell when he gets home. Mom says you're going to be taking care of him."

"If he'll let me."

A grin formed on Gerald's lips. "Oh, I'm sure he'll let you. He'll be an ass, but he'll let you."

"You're all being very kind to me. I'm not sure why."

"You're family," he said standing. "You always have been." He moved back to the doorway and turned around. "I'm headed into town. Do you need anything?"

"I'd love to get your parents something for Christmas. I don't know what, but…"

"Can you still make that pumpkin pie you used to make?"

She chuckled. "Well, yes."

"I'll get the ingredients for that. Text them to me. Mom would love that for Christmas."

"Oh, that's not enough."

"Sure it is. She has Santa coming this year too. You have no idea the joy you're bringing her. We'll keep you safe, and you'll be giving Mom something she's been yearning for."

"You know, Russ might kick me out."

"No. He'd never put you in harm's way. Phillip seems to think you're in it. He'll be happy to have you here, even if he doesn't act like it." With a wink, he turned and left.

She stood there a moment and laughed when she thought about the pie. Seriously, she could not repay them with dessert.

In time she would find a way. For now, she was going to enjoy the moment. She was part of a family again—the family she'd always wanted to be part of.

RUSSELL LAY in his hospital bed, free of wire and tubes, except for the stupid catheter they thought he needed since some shard of glass had stabbed him. He still had stitches, bandages, and of course the stupid bandage that took up all of his leg. But the doctor had given him release, and now he just waited for the nurse to finish the paperwork.

His mother sat in the chair next to his bed with an enormous grin on her face, and his father paced, as he normally did.

He couldn't deny that he was ready to go home, but he knew

what waited for him. His mother hadn't stopped talking about Chelsea and her son since she'd walked in that morning.

There was some surprise that his blood pressure had been fine. He'd been stressing over Chelsea for the past two days. Even more, he was nervous to see her son for the first time. There was something finite in knowing he'd been born of a bond that had torn Russell's world apart.

Pettiness didn't sit well with him. The feeling that he couldn't quite let it go irritated him. In fact, he'd had to control his breathing so that he wouldn't alarm anyone.

He didn't want to be mad at Chelsea anymore. She had a lot on her plate. Certainly, he didn't want to hold a grudge against some three-year-old either.

It was going to take some work, but he was willing to have an open mind. After all, his mother was ecstatic for Christmas morning with a toddler in the house.

"I remember when you boys would walk down the stairs and see the Christmas tree. You and Ben would plan all year for Santa's arrival. Gerald and Dane were a little leerier of him. Eric, well he was just a good sport for so long." She opened her purse and took out her lipstick, applied it, and returned it to her purse. "I know Lucas is going to enjoy Santa this year. He and I made two batches of cookies. Well," she laughed, "we ate the first batch."

"I'm sure Chelsea appreciates all you're doing."

She took a breath to say something else, but the nurse walked in causing his mother's excitement to shift.

"Mr. Walker, you're all set to go home." She handed him a stack of papers. "Here is your discharge information. Your appointments are all made and listed on the last sheet. Your mother assured us you'd have some home care. That'll help in your recovery. Of course, there will be no walking. When you come back for your visit, and they remove the staples from your surgery, they can assess you then and decide on your recovery.

Until then, you'll keep your leg elevated and bandaged as it is now."

"How long will that be?" He wanted out of it now.

"A few more weeks. Mind your nurse, and you'll heal faster," she said with a wink.

Russell gritted his teeth. How had it come to be that his healing and his return to normality would depend on the one woman who stole all of that in the first place?

He was helped into a wheelchair and out to his mother's car. Even though he wasn't thrilled about what awaited him at home, he knew his father couldn't drive fast enough, because home was right where he wanted to be.

CHAPTER 9

Susan scurried around the kitchen with Lydia in tow prepping dinner. Eric had come through the back door and stolen food from the tray his wife had set out, which had given her reason to slap his hand.

Dane walked in with Gia, after having picked her up at the airport. She'd been in Everett Walker's office making phone calls since she'd said hello to everyone.

Gerald, Ben, and Dane now joined Eric in the kitchen, and they all paced as if they didn't know what to do with themselves.

Chelsea sat at the table with Lucas while he ate his snack. She was surprised that he was eating from a plate of cut up snacks Susan had made for him. Perhaps living with the Walkers would be good for him. Chelsea certainly wasn't culinary, and Lucas needed a broader food base, that was for sure.

But, she thought, at least it kept her from joining everyone and pacing the room. She was more nervous than she could remember. Even more so than when she'd first been standing in Russell's hospital room, holding his arm, taking his vitals when he'd awoken that first morning.

How they possibly heard the car driving up to the house

amongst the chatter going on in the kitchen, she had no idea, but the entire family dropped whatever they were doing and headed to the front door.

Chelsea sat at the table, Lucas still on her lap. She was paralyzed in the chair. It wasn't appropriate for her to run to the door. She shouldn't be excited to see him come into the house. Fear had her sick, knowing he was going to have that scowl on his face that meant he wasn't happy to see her. Why would he be?

Lucas squirmed on her lap until he managed out of her arms and ran off toward the door. How was it she couldn't even keep up with a toddler?

She followed him out to where everyone gathered outside the door. He pushed through their legs and ran straight to Glenda.

"Oh, look who came to greet us." She picked Lucas up and rested him on her hip as Gerald pushed the wheelchair to the car and helped Russell out.

WHEN RUSSELL HAD RETURNED from the service, he'd received much of the same greeting he was receiving now. Only then, it was just his brothers. He noticed Susan was standing next to Eric, and Dane stood with his arm around Gia. Lydia Morgan had moved in front of the group, and Ben had rested his hands on her shoulders.

Gerald had moved in and helped balance him as he managed his way out of the car and into the wheelchair, which was now his norm.

As Gerald turned him from the car, he got his first glimpse of the boy he'd been thinking of. Chelsea's son had run outside and right to Glenda, who had scooped him up and planted a kiss right on his cheek.

"I guess he was eager to meet you," she said as she walked toward him. "This is our guest, Lucas."

The little boy buried his face in Russell's mother's neck. "He seems to like you."

"Of course, he does. I'm loveable," she agreed.

He looked at the boy—studied him as he raised his head. Blond hair, blue eyes, and a familiar smile gazed down at him. He looked like his mother, and that eased the pain he was having in his chest.

As Gerald pushed him toward the house, each of his brothers and their significant others shook his hand, patted him on the back, or kissed his cheek.

Lydia jumped right in front of his chair, placed her hands on his cheeks, and gave him a generous kiss on the lips.

"I'm so glad you're home. You will heal so much better here. And then when you're ready..."

He laughed. "I can help you with your new place."

"Absolutely." She kissed him again before stepping to the side.

Just as Gerald pushed him to the door, Chelsea stepped into view. "Welcome home," she said, with as much trepidation as he was feeling.

"Thanks." His voice cracked as he spoke. How was this possibly going to work, when both of them were so obviously uncomfortable?

"I'd better get Lucas, so your mom can get you settled."

She started by him, and he reached for her. "He looks just like you," he said, hoping the sincerity relayed correctly.

"He's my life." Though her words should have sliced right through his heart, seeing her there, and having seen him, he knew the extent of her love for her son. It was admirable, especially considering his paternity.

She slid by them, and Gerald pushed him into the house, through to the kitchen where it looked as though they were having a party.

"What's all this?" he asked.

"They're all excited to have you home. So if you need to rest, you'd better let me know. You know how this family is, this could go on for hours," Gerald joked at their family's expense.

Russell chuckled. "I know I'm supposed to rest, but I think this might be what I need for the moment."

CHELSEA REACHED for Lucas and pulled him to her. "He's going to do much better at home," she told Glenda, who watched her family file into the house.

"I know he will. It'll surprise everyone."

"Would you mind if I took Lucas out back and showed him the chickens?"

Glenda's brows drew together. "Now? Don't you want to come in and eat?"

"I think I need a few minutes to collect myself. I'm just a little overwhelmed."

Glenda rubbed her arm. "Take all the time you need. Our home and our land is yours. He should explore and enjoy every part of it."

Chelsea watched Glenda follow her family back into the house. She took a deep breath and gave Lucas a kiss on the forehead. "Would you like to see the chickens?"

"Chick-in," he replied as he wiggled out of her arms and down her body. He started off, stopped and held his hand out for her, and waited for her to catch up. "Chick-in, Mommy."

She wondered if there would ever be a time when she didn't nearly tear up when he called her *Mommy*. How could it tug at her heart still? But it did.

RUSSELL WATCHED Chelsea and Lucas from the back door. Lucas had a lot of energy, and she had a genuine smile to match. Russell had been prepared for it to hurt when he saw them together, but even he could admit, he'd never made her as happy as she was just looking at the chickens with her son.

"He loves his mommy," his mother said as she set a plate of food on the table next to him.

"I didn't know what to expect when I saw him—or her here for that matter."

"She needs us, and you need her," his mother sat down next to him. "Be open minded."

"I'll do my best," he said with a hint of sarcasm. Then he relaxed in his chair. "I'll admit, I'm not sure what my mood will be now that I'm home. Sitting in this damn chair only pisses me off."

"It's part of your recovery. Be strong of mind and you'll recover physically," she offered as she took a piece of cheese from the plate she'd brought him and popped it into her mouth.

"I shouldn't be in this chair at all," he said, turning to face her. "I wasn't drunk that night. I don't remember losing control of my truck. I don't remember anyone running me off the road either."

"But Phillip said you were, and they found the truck that did it."

He nodded. "He told me. Her ex-husband's truck."

"And it was parked outside of her house," his mother whispered as if it were a secret.

Russell rubbed the ache starting between his eyes. It didn't sit right with him. Who was at the bar that night in another blue truck? And he hadn't known anyone at the bar either.

"You're due for your pain meds." She stood from the table and hurried off to find the bag they'd brought home as Chelsea and Lucas came through the back door. She had hold of both his hands and walked behind him. He was covered in mud and grinning from ear to ear.

Russell's mother walked back to the table with the pills she'd gone after, and a glass of water. Shifting a glance at Chelsea she tucked in a smile. "Oh, my goodness. What happened here?"

"Lucas seems to think it's a fun game to chase the chickens," she said still holding tightly to his hands. "I need to throw him in a tub, but I don't want to get mud all over the house."

"I'll get him some clean clothes, and you take him into Russell's room. There's a tub in there."

Russell swallowed the pills his mother had given him and nearly choked on them. "My room doesn't have a bathroom."

"Honey, we moved you down to the main level. It'll be a bit before you can do the stairs. Chelsea and Lucas are staying in your room."

The panicked look on Chelsea's face meant that the reaction to his mother's words had left a trail of irritation on his.

"We'll hurry," Chelsea said as she hurried past them to the bedroom down the hall from the kitchen.

His mother sat back down next to him. The pain was building, but behind his eyes and not in his leg or arm. His mother put her hand on his arm. "You should lie down."

"Seems as though my room is being occupied," he quipped through gritted teeth.

"I'll go help her."

"Don't bother. No need to hurry her," he said on a breath. "I'm going to just roll myself in there and lay down."

"I'll help you then."

"I don't need help," he snapped and realized he'd done so loudly, as everyone turned and grew quiet.

That was when the excuses started, and his family began to dismiss themselves one by one. Soon it was just him and his mother, alone in the kitchen. The headache had compounded, and a niggling thought was itching in his brain.

He hadn't meant to be so sour about everything. Getting home was supposed to have made everything better.

His mother had escorted everyone out the door and then run upstairs after the clothes she'd promised Chelsea she'd find.

It was then Russell noticed that even his father had somehow exited with the crowd. He was sitting there absolutely alone.

He could use this against them when he was pissed.

Backing his chair away from the table, he managed to maneuver it through the kitchen without crashing his extended leg into anything. Navigating the turn to the hall was a little trickier, especially since he only, really, had one good arm.

He managed himself into the guestroom on the main level. Sounds of water, a small voice singing, and Chelsea's voice soothing came from the bathroom.

For a moment he let himself enjoy the sounds. Once he'd wanted a house full of them. Chances were that would never happen. He'd grown too crabby and undesirable. There were times he couldn't even stand himself.

Russell rolled the wheelchair to the side of the bed. Pulling back the bedding, he exposed the fancy linens his mother would save for guests. If he had to recover there, he might as well enjoy the best his mother had to offer.

Putting the brakes on the chair, Russell carefully bent to move the foot plates. Every muscle in his body still ached. Even these tedious tasks hurt. But he'd be damned if it was going to hold him back.

Once he removed the obstacles, he pushed up with his good arm, to stand on his good leg. Even that was wobbly, but the bed was only a few inches away. He could do this.

Pushing harder, he got up on one leg, but the brakes on the chair weren't as secure as he'd thought.

Just as Chelsea walked out of the bathroom with the toddler in her arms wrapped in a towel, Russell felt the chair move, and he was headed toward the floor.

It all flashed before him. He was going down. Then he saw the little boy running around naked, and two strong, yet feminine arms were wrapped around him keeping him from falling.

"What in the hell were you doing?" Chelsea hollered as she

guided him toward the bed, and sat him on the edge. "You could have fallen and hurt yourself."

"I'm already hurt."

"Don't you get sassy with me," she scolded. Her cheeks were fire red, and her eyes wide. "I'm here to help you, and you're damn well going to let me. Don't you ever do that again."

"You're not my mother," he retorted with equal venom.

"No, but I am," his mother said from the doorway as she picked up Lucas and wrapped him back up in his towel. "I'll strap you to that bed if you do that again."

Russell fisted his hands. "I'm fine. I have to learn to do this."

Chelsea leaned in real close. "Then you let me teach you," she growled through clenched teeth. "I'll damn well let you do it when you're strong enough."

His mother cleared her throat. "I'll take him upstairs and get him dressed."

He noticed Chelsea didn't even look their way. "Thank you," she said as she kept a steely stare on him. When his mother and her son were out of the room, she eased back. "As pleasant as it is, why don't you let me look at your catheter bag so I can dump it."

Humiliation crept up his spine and spread through his skin like a burn from the inside. "Can't we have someone else do that?"

"I'm the nurse your parents hired to take care of you."

"But you're not a full nurse yet."

"Nope, but I'm here. It'll take them hours to get someone else out here from town to do it. By then, you might have an infection if its full and flowing the wrong way up the tube. Perhaps you should just remember that I've seen everything you have, only now it's absolutely in a professional capacity. You don't have to worry about anything."

God, he hated this. He hated every part of it.

He had no choices. This was his reality.

"Fine," he spat out. "Do it and then let me get some rest. Those pills my mother gave me are starting to make your face fuzzy."

She laughed as she lifted his legs onto the bed and pulled up his pant leg.

Russell laid his head back on the billion pillows his mother thought the bed needed for show, and closed his eyes. He didn't want to see her looking at his—anything.

She lifted his pant leg only. "You'll be okay for a little bit. What this tells me is you need more fluids."

He opened his eyes and squinted at her. "These are not the kinds of things I want to hear you tell me."

"Oh, is there anything you want me to tell you?" She bore a stare into him, and he knew she was thinking about his drugged slip of words when he'd first seen her. He'd told her he loved her, and he wondered if it would always haunt him. But then he thought about it. There was something he wanted her to tell him.

"Why don't you tell me where you were the night of my accident."

Her eyes grew wide. "You want to know where I was when you were in your accident?"

"Yeah. I mean, I was run off the road by a truck that was owned by your ex-husband, which they found parked at your house."

"Across from my house," she clarified curtly.

"Did he leave you that truck?"

Chelsea fisted her hands at her side, and he could see the lines form at the corners of her eyes. Her breath came faster now, and he was finding great satisfaction in seeing her fume over his question.

"I have never driven that truck before."

"So, where were you?"

Her nostrils were flaring and he'd yet to get his answer. Was she having to think about it? Could he possibly have hit on something?

"Is everything okay," his mother's voice cut through the tension that had enveloped the room

She stepped in with Lucas on her hip, but the moment he saw his mother, he wiggled his way down and hurried to Chelsea.

She batted her eyes, obviously trying not to cry. Lucas pulled at her pant leg, and she bent down to pick him up.

"A nurse will be here in the morning. I'll have her check in on you," she informed him gruffly.

His mother moved toward the bed. "Is everything okay here?"

"I'll let him fill you in. I'm going to go pack." She turned toward his mother. "Thank you again for everything. This isn't going to work."

A moment later she was gone.

His mother fisted her hands on her hips, narrowed her stare on him, and moved in. He might be a grown man, but she still scared the hell out of him. The only difference between when he was a child and now—he couldn't run.

"What did you say to her."

"Mom, it's not worth it. I don't know what you're thinking to have her here helping me, but…"

"I'm helping her. You'll be fine soon enough," she interrupted. "That girl needs someone to watch over her. Phillip can't do it all the time. He's protecting the rest of the city. That little boy doesn't need any more drama in his short little life. He needs love. He needs fresh air. He needs chicken coops to get muddy in. You…you need to focus on healing. And I can't think of a better way than having someone who knows how to put up with your whiney crap help you along."

His mouth fell open, but he had no words.

How could he have accused her of hurting him physically? Sure, she'd done it emotionally. Then again, who says she couldn't have done it anyway.

The drugs were messing up his thinking. Hell, a few days ago, he'd told the woman he loved her. Could it be any more confusing?

Russell looked at his mother, but she was getting fuzzy. The pain meds she'd given him were starting to take effect. There needed to be an apology. He just wasn't sure if it should come to him or if he should be giving it. It took a lot of through process to realize it was dark. His eyes were closed and for the life of him, he couldn't pry them open.

The swirling in his head usually meant he was going under. Fine, he'd face this problem when he woke up. At least he'd have more energy for it then.

CHAPTER 10

*L*ucas had begun to cry when Chelsea took his blanket and shoved it in the suitcase. At the moment, she had to turn a deaf ear to it and finish what she'd started. They needed to get out of the house and go back to their life—the one that didn't include the Walkers, no matter how depressing the thought.

When she picked up his Tigger, he let out an ungodly screech, and she turned to see him standing there with his arms up and his face red from the tears he'd been crying.

This wasn't what she'd wanted when she'd stormed out on Russell. She'd wanted Russell to look like this.

Chelsea picked up Lucas and handed him the Tigger. Then she pulled him close to her, and he rested his head on her shoulder, almost as if he knew she needed the comfort.

There was a knock at the door, and when she looked up, she saw Phillip standing there, his hat in his hand.

"Glenda says our patient is a little testy."

She realized she was rocking from side to side as Lucas had fallen asleep on her shoulder. Perhaps his falling asleep was to calm her as much as it was what he needed.

Because she wasn't going to wake him, she took a breath and quieted her voice. "He's an ass. I can't do this. I can't stay here and take care of him." She rubbed Lucas's back as she walked toward the bed. With his Tigger gripped tightly in his hands, she laid him down on the bed and pulled a small blanket up over him.

Phillip moved in behind her and looked down at him. "He's precious, Chelsea. Makes me wish I'd have had one."

"Why didn't you?"

"My choice in women that I married was never good."

"You still have time."

He chuckled quietly. "Only got eyes on one woman, and I find a way to seem like the idiot I have a reputation for being, when-ever she's around." Backing up, he ran his hand over the rim of his hat. "Listen, I know you're not happy here, but you need to stay out here."

"I'll be fine at home. I don't…"

"Your house was broken into last night."

Chelsea felt the tightness in her chest, and her breath grew thick in her lungs. Gently, she sat down on the bed next to Lucas, who continued to sleep soundly.

"Dominic?"

Patrick shook his head. "Still have eyes on him in Texas, and he's right where he's supposed to be."

"Who's doing this?"

"I don't know. We took the truck in, and we're trying to iden-tify who was driving it."

She hated being in such a vulnerable position. Feeling hunted was a horrible feeling. Chelsea shifted her eyes up to look at Phillip. "I don't want anything to happen to the Walkers. They don't deserve to have anything happen to them because of me. I need to find somewhere else for Lucas and me. If this is someone who knows me, they'll look for me with my parents and my sister. I don't want them hurt either."

"The safest place for you is here. No one is going to let anyone near you."

"Why would they do this for me?"

"You're worth it, Chels. This family has a high tolerance for pain if you will. Nothing will break them."

She knew that was true. The Walkers never let anything break them. Not family feuds. Not greedy land grabbers. Not possessive ex-cops. They were forgiving and decent people.

"I'll stay," she said softly. "I'll take care of Russ, and I'll stay."

Phillip smiled. "Good. He needs you, and you need them. It's as if it were fate."

"Someone's sick idea of fate."

He nodded. "If you can think of any reason someone wants in your house, you let me know. I walked through, and I don't see anything out of place from when we were there."

"I feel violated."

"That might be all they were going for. But you think about it, and you stay here. Everett and the boys know what's going on, and I've even talked to Byron Walker to see if he knows anything. You know, if there's something bad going down around here, he's usually got a hand in it."

She couldn't help but let a little laugh slip. Byron Walker was known for being mischievous and backhanded. "He knew nothing?"

"Nope, but he's keeping his ears open too."

"Thank you," she said reaching up and touching his arm. "You have no idea how much all this means to me."

"Just doing my job." He turned and walked toward the door before turning back. "Ya, know, if you ever need an extra hand with him, you might ask Lydia Morgan. She's fantastic with kids," he said and then walked out the door.

Chelsea smiled as she thought of what he'd said. *Only ever had eyes on one woman, and I find a way to seem like the idiot I have a reputation for being, whenever she's around.* To anyone it would have to be completely obvious who he'd been talking about. The only one that was that oblivious, she thought, was Lydia.

Maybe she could talk to her about him. After all, he seemed to be very vested in keeping her safe. Perhaps it was the least she could do for him.

Lucas stirred next to her, and she looked down at him. He was her miracle, and she loved him more than she ever could have imagined she'd love anyone.

Feeling the strain of the day, she laid down next to him and closed her eyes. She, too, could use a little refreshing nap.

RUSSELL WOKE in his own room, but it had taken him a moment even to realize where he was. He needed to focus on getting stronger because those pain meds weren't worth the hangover.

He sat up and managed to scoot himself into a position where he was comfortable on the bed. His left arm was sore, and he took the sling off of it and tried to move it.

It hurt like a bitch, but he'd focus on getting it back to normal. That would help him when they let him walk. He knew he'd have to use crutches for a while, so he might as well get that upper body strong.

The door to his room opened, and he looked up assuming he'd see his mother or Chelsea walk through. He hoped for Chelsea. He owed her an apology.

Instead, a woman in scrubs with little penguins walked into the room with a glass of water and a little cup of pills.

"Hello, Russell. I'm Karen. I'm here to check up on you," she said as she handed him the glass and the pills.

"Where's Chelsea?"

"She's only a student. She's here to help you when you don't have a nurse here. I'm here to oversee your care and supervise her."

He looked at his hand. "What are these."

"Simply some Tylenol."

"Good. I don't want that other stuff. I don't like them."

She nodded. "Yes, but it keeps your pain down."

"I'm fine with pain. I'd rather get over this and get back on my feet."

She smiled in a way that told him she heard that all the time, but he truly meant it. He hated the thought of his brothers picking up his slack. There was no reason he couldn't do some of his own work around the ranch. He'd talk to them about it. For a bit, he'd need to do things closer to the house and easier for him to get to in his wheelchair, but he could do something.

Never did he think he'd be begging for chores, but he felt as though not only his body was suffering but so was his mind.

Karen turned toward the dresser and opened a bag he'd never seen before. She took out a blood pressure cuff and a stethoscope and walked back to him.

"Let's see how you're doing." She put the cuff on his arm and adjusted it.

"So Chelsea is still here? She's still going to work with me?"

"Uh-huh," she said as she put the pieces of the stethoscope in her ears.

He waited until she'd pumped up the cuff, let the air out, and removed the stethoscope from her ears before he spoke again. "She didn't quit?"

"Well, I've only been here a few hours. I talked to her, and she didn't mention it."

"So she's still in the house?"

Karen took the cuff from his arm and placed both items back in her bag. "She was feeding her son when I saw her last. It didn't look as if she were going anywhere."

He let the tension in his shoulders ease when she said it.

"What do you say to getting bathed?" she asked and the

tension formed again. "The shower stool is in place. I'll get some wrap for your incision and we'll get you cleaned up."

He only nodded, but the thought that this would normally be part of Chelsea's job filled him with mixed emotions. When his heart rate kicked up, he realized that the excited emotion had won over.

Russell knew he was a horrible patient. His mother had told him that most of his life. Knowing that his accusation had hurt Chelsea, he decided he'd work on being a little more cordial. After all, if he weren't, he'd never get out of that bed on his own and he'd have Karen giving him a shower for the rest of his life.

CHAPTER 11

*A*s a man, Russell could easily fantasize about a woman giving him a shower, and he'd been known to. But he was fairly sure that having Karen shower him might have ruined all his fantasies.

Before Karen had left, she'd gotten him dressed, helped him into his wheelchair, and taken him out to the kitchen where his mother was cooking dinner.

"You look fresh," his mother said as Karen let herself out.

"I feel better. But I'll admit, I'll be happier when I can shower myself," he chuckled and reached up onto the counter to take an apple from a bowl.

He set the apple in his lap and managed around the island with one hand.

"Who will be eating with us?" he asked as he took a bite of the apple.

"Dad, Gerald, and Ben are finishing up that shed out on the far west field. So I'm going to take this out to them. With Gia back, Dane is staying in town with her."

"One less mouth for you to feed."

She shrugged. "I'm happy when my boys move on, but I miss having them at my dinner table."

Of course, she hadn't mentioned the names he'd been hoping for, yet she'd said she was leaving to take dinner out to the others. She was setting him up to ask, so he might as well take her bait.

"Where are Chelsea and Lucas?"

She didn't answer right away and continued putting together the meal she'd been working on.

Finally, she lifted her eyes to him, and he could see they were pained and a bit misty. "Lucas wanted to go see the chickens again. She put him in the old wagon in the garage hoping to keep him from the mud."

"So they're still here."

His mother set the spoon she'd been using down on the counter and braced her hands on either side of the bowl in which she'd been stirring.

This was a stance he'd grown accustomed to in his teenage years, but he'd have to admit, he hadn't seen it in a very long time. He was about to get his ass chewed, and he was a fully grown man.

"I'm very surprised you're even asking about her, the way you dismissed her and all."

"I was wrong," he said as sympathetically as he could, trying to divert the storm about to come.

"Damn straight you were. You had no right to accuse her of being the one who drove you off the road."

"I didn't say that." He held up a hand in protest.

When she turned, he saw the fire in his mother's eyes, and he knew she'd understood the context just fine—correct words or not.

"You know that's what you were asking her. How could you possibly think she had anything to do with what happened to you?"

"All of this seems to have a strange underlying coincidence, which doesn't have anything to do with me, but has a whole lot to do with her."

He could see his mother's jaw tense. "That may be the case, but just coincidence." Her eyes went sympathetic. "Someone is messing with her. I suppose if they knew you were an important part of her life, then..."

"But I wasn't. She left me and moved on. I haven't been a part of her life in years, Mom. Why would someone hurt me because of our past when we weren't connected now?"

Her shoulders dropped. "I don't know, honey. I just don't want to see her hurt, or that sweet baby. I know she hurt you—deeply—but I can't turn her away."

Russell let out a breath. "I don't want her to go either. I'll try to be a better patient and stay calm."

"When it's over, and you're back on your feet, then you two can decide your own path."

With his right leg, he pushed the chair toward her and looked up at her. "Mom, I'll do this for her, because I once cared for her. But there is no path for us. I can't trust her with my heart, no matter what I might have felt."

He swore he saw a tear in her eye, but it vanished as she nodded and went back to stirring the pot. There was more she wanted to say, and he knew that. But she refrained.

Russell backed himself up and maneuvered his way to the table as his mother packed up the dinner she'd made for his father and brothers.

Before she headed out, she informed him that there were three places set for him, Chelsea, and Lucas. She'd be eating with the others.

A few moments later, Chelsea and Lucas walked into the kitchen. Lucas ran straight to the back door and pressed his nose to the glass.

Chelsea chuckled. "He's obsessed with the chickens and the

horses. Eric took him for a short ride today," she said, as if only making small talk.

"It's a perfect place for a little boy."

She nodded as she picked up the plates his mother had left for them. She placed one in front of Russell and another next to him, then went back for the other.

"C'mon, Lucas. Mrs. Walker made you spaghetti."

"Yum," he called out, and hurried to her. As he approached the table, he stopped and looked up at Russell. There was no crying or laughing, no talking or pointing, he only stared.

Russell smiled, but Lucas didn't return it.

"I don't think he likes me," he said as Chelsea picked Lucas up and set him on her lap.

"He just doesn't know you yet, and your face is still bruised," she assured him as she kissed her son's head and began to work around him to get his food ready for him.

"If you're going to be staying, looks like we need to get him a highchair."

She lifted her head and met his eye with a hesitant stare. "We're staying."

Russell nodded. "You should stay. I was wrong to talk to you like I did earlier."

Chelsea gave Lucas a breadstick, and he bit into it while she kept a steely eye on Russell. "You're admitting you were wrong? I don't think I've ever heard you..."

"Stop," he said with a wince. "I know I don't admit to being wrong—ever. But I was. You have no reason to have hurt me physically."

"Because I already hurt you, emotionally?"

"Did you want to fight?" he asked feeling the tension between them building.

Chelsea shook her head and then ran a hand over Lucas's hair. "No. I don't want to fight. I'm grateful for what your family is doing for us. Being here to help you recover is the only thing I can do to repay them for their generosity." She looked down at the plate just to her side. She picked up her fork and twirled the noodles on it, then set it down. "Someone broke into my house after Phillip and I were there last."

"What are they looking for?"

"I don't know," her voice dipped, and he watched her bat away a tear. "Russ, he kidnapped Lucas once. What if he's planning it again? What if…"

He reached his hand to her arm, which held Lucas, and touched her gently. "Sweetheart, nothing is going to happen to him. I'll see to it personally."

"Why?"

Because I love you, were the words that rang in his head, but he sure as hell wasn't going down that path again. He was sober and not on any drugs at the moment. "I care for you," he said, settling on the words. "We may not have the future we'd once planned, but I wish you no ill will. And he doesn't deserve to grow up with his mother afraid."

Lucas picked up the second breadstick on his plate and held it out to Russell. "You eat," he said and lifted the stick toward him.

"That one's yours. I have some."

"You eat this," he said again, urging Russell to take it.

The tears had dried in her eyes now, and love lit in them. It stung. She used to look at him like she looked at Lucas.

Russell took the breadstick. "Thank you." He then picked up the one on his plate and handed it to Lucas. "Here, you have this one."

Lucas grabbed it and held it to him. He looked up at his mother and smiled wide.

They'd had a moment of bonding. Russell would take it. It was warm and comforting to him, and because of the feelings that were stirring inside of him, he wanted to continue to have moments like the one they were sharing. That would only happen if he could keep his mouth in check and his attitude calm.

. . .

CHELSEA WAS MAKING a mental list of things she needed from her house. The highchair was one of them. Perhaps she could have Dane or Gerald take her into town, and they could stop by her house. Surely Phillip would approve of that if she weren't alone.

She'd like to have one of the baby gates and Lucas's toddler bed too. They'd been making some potty training progress until they'd been displaced. She'd have to start all over again, but that was okay. But his potty was at the house too.

"Are you going to eat that?" Russell asked, and she realized she was only spinning her noodles on her fork, not actually eating.

"My mind is in other places."

Lucas pushed away his plate and began to wiggle in her lap as though he were fighting to get down.

"Oh, no you don't," she argued with him. "You're a mess, and Mrs. Walker doesn't need you running around here like that."

She picked him up just as Glenda Walker walked back into the house with the box she'd taken with her to feed the others.

"Well, look who ate dinner." She moved toward them and reached her hands out to take Lucas. "That makes me feel good. Did you like dinner?"

He nodded and then pointed to Russell. "He eat my dinner."

Russell held his hand in surrender. "It was a gift."

Chelsea laughed. "I'll get him cleaned up. You don't want him right now. He's a mess."

Glenda urged her with a wave. "I'll take him, and we'll get cleaned up. Nothing would make me happier." She pulled Lucas to her and gave him a kiss on the head. She then looked between Chelsea and Russell. "I think he has some pain meds due soon."

"In twenty minutes," Chelsea assured her.

"Good. We're going to go clean up, and then play a little if that's okay with you."

A warmth spread through her and Chelsea smiled. "Of course. Thank you."

"Oh, no. Thank you," Glenda said, as she carried him away.

Chelsea watched her carry him off, and a part of her wanted to cry from the sadness that he loved spending time with someone other than her. The other half was emotionally grateful that Lucas had someone like Glenda to love him. Her mother wasn't close and Dominic's mother—well, that thought alone scared the hell out of her.

She was a nasty woman whom Chelsea had hardly known. Even Dominic was afraid of her, and he didn't fear anything—obviously. She'd been the mastermind behind Dominic taking Lucas in the first place. It was her evil plan to keep what she thought what was hers and hurt Chelsea just as she'd felt her son had been hurt.

"You do see what's going on, don't you," Russell spoke again, snapping her from her trance. "You're worried about your ex-husband, but my mother has kidnapped you both," he said smiling.

"Doesn't seem so bad." She laughed as she walked back to the table and picked up her plate and Lucas's.

"Why don't you sit and eat now? You've gotten skinny. I assume this is why. He eats, and you clean."

"I should…"

"You should sit down, finish your dinner, and we could have a real conversation before you give me those stupid pills."

She contemplated his offer for just a moment before sitting down next to him and eating the cold plate of spaghetti.

She was so consumed with eating that it took her a while to realize that Russell was sitting there staring at her.

"What?" she asked, her mouth full of spaghetti.

"I've missed this."

"Staring at me?" She swallowed, and then wiped her mouth.

Russell chuckled. "Yeah, that too. But I meant I missed us sitting together, being civil."

Chelsea moved her food around again, something she realized she did when she was horribly nervous. "Russ, I'm sorry again that I…"

"Don't," he said reaching for her hand and holding it in his.

She gasped at the feel of his skin on hers. His thumb brushed her knuckles. It was so very familiar, and yet so removed that it felt new.

"I can't help it," she continued. "This is all my fault. All of it. I hurt you. I hurt your family. I hurt my own heart," she rambled on. "Now you're hurt, and I'm hiding. This is horrible."

"Scoot closer," he said, giving her hand a tug.

"Russ…"

"C'mon. I'm not going to yell at you," he promised.

Chelsea moved her chair, and he adjusted his so that they were as close as they could get. He lifted his hand to her face and caressed her cheek. "I think we should call a truce."

"O-kay," she let the word release slowly. "You're going to let me take care of you?"

"After Karen gave me my shower, I'm looking forward to it." He smiled, and it caused her to laugh.

"You always liked taking showers with women," she joked.

"Just you," his tone had changed again, and she felt his words heavy on her chest.

"Russ, we can't talk like this."

"Yes, we can. We have a past. We had a great past."

"Until I messed it up," she threw it in there again, and he eased back.

"Fine." He dropped his hand from hers. "Do you want me to say it? You messed it up. You took something good and threw it away. Does that make you feel better?"

"No," she bit back and then swallowed the tears that were threatening.

Russell took her hand again, this time lacing their fingers together. "We started out as friends. Do you remember that?"

Chelsea nodded. It was a fond memory—one she drew from in some of her saddest times.

"Let's start there. I want to be your friend. You need a friend, Chels. You need me."

Oh, she could go on and argue again that she'd caused all the problems that now faced them, but they were both aware of them. For now, she'd accept his truce.

"Okay. I'd like to stay here with all of you, and help get you back on your feet. And," she took a deep breath, "I think it will be a good thing to have Lucas around good role models."

"Can't find better ones than right here," he said, and she knew he meant his father and his brothers—but her mind went straight to him as the perfect role model for her son.

She let her eyes sink into his as she bit down on her bottom lip. "That's exactly what I was thinking."

CHAPTER 12

*R*ussell spent a few hours in his father's office after dinner. The pain meds Chelsea had given him hadn't affected him quite as badly as they had before. He was still awake and alert. He liked that much better. Perhaps she'd begun to wean him from the full dosage. If that was the case, he was all for it.

Lydia had emailed him pictures of her new house, which she was looking forward to having him help her fix up. He liked knowing he'd have some purpose when he was back up on his feet. He jotted down some notes from looking at the pictures. There were some items she needed to attend to before he could even get to her.

Looking at the house made him think about the plans he and Chelsea had once made, so many years ago. His father had promised each of them a piece of the land to build their houses on. He'd always wanted a small house on the far west corner of the family property, about two miles further west than Eric.

There was room for a house of any size, but he always thought that a small house could be added on to, if they chose, but really, who needed a big house when they had endless acres right out the front door?

He'd never needed anything as a child when it came to the room to play. They'd had an above ground pool, which had ceased to go up when they'd all become too old. There were roads to ride bicycles and dirt bikes on. Streams ran through the property where they'd all fished, swam, and skipped rocks. Groves of trees provided hours of climbing and hiding. The possibilities were endless.

The thoughts brought a smile to his lips.

He typed a search into Google for prefabricated houses. He'd watched a show on it when he was in the hospital, and he'd been very impressed. Order a house and they deliver. Seriously, what was easier than that?

"You're not surfing porn on my computer are you," his father's voice broke through the silence, and Russell jumped.

"Right. As if I am dumb enough to do that."

His father shrugged, as if to toy with him. "What are you doing? You look good by the way."

"I feel good. I'll be perfect when I can get out of this chair."

"In time," his father said as he walked around the desk. "Houses? Ready to stake your claim, huh?"

"I'm thinking about it. I was watching a show on these prefabricated houses and thought that would be an excellent place to start. Then the sky's the limit."

His father patted him on the back. "We can drive up to Athens and take a look when you're feeling up to it," he offered.

"I'd like that."

"Maybe after the new year."

"Hey, are you busy tomorrow? I'd like to go to town and do some Christmas shopping for Lucas and Chelsea."

His father raised an eyebrow. "You want to buy them gifts?"

He nodded his head. "Yeah. I don't see a future for us, but I see a friendship. So I might as well be a good friend."

A smile formed on his father's lips. "I think that's nice. Are you allowed to go to town?"

Russell ran his tongue over his teeth. "Not sure that I am, but what if we just tell them we're checking fencelines, and you're getting me out of the house for a bit."

Now his father laughed. "If your mother finds out…"

"You can buy her something special while we're out then."

The laughter continued as his father rested a hand on his shoulder just as his mother walked into the office.

"Are you ready?" she asked, and Russell looked up at his father.

"You going out?"

"Nah, I have something to show you," he said before exchanging smiles with Russell's mother.

Russell unlocked the wheels of the chair, and his father guided him out from behind the desk and to the hallway. He then pushed him to the front door where his brothers all stood as well as Chelsea and Lucas.

There was a ramp where the stairs were, and he could feel tears burn his throat.

"You made me a ramp?" he choked out the words.

"We made you three. There's one out the back and one into the garage."

Russell cleared his throat. "Is this what you were working on?"

Eric laughed. "We've been working on them for the past few days in the barn up at my house. You're not one to stay in the house. We thought this would make your recovery easier if you could get out a bit."

He covered his mouth. He wasn't going to cry, he promised. There was too much hell to be had, with all of his brothers standing around him. But before he fell asleep, he'd shed a tear or two in appreciation. That was acceptable—alone—in the dark.

His father leaned in, with his hands on the back of the chair. "Ready for your first spin? I'll take you down it, but it should be just the right angle when you get that sling off your arm you'll be able to do it with ease."

"I'm ready," he said.

Slowly, his father took him down the ramp, and they all whooped at their success. Russell couldn't say it was a gift he'd ever had wanted, but it just might have been the best one.

"Me turn. Me." Lucas wiggled down his mother's body and toward Russell.

Chelsea ran after him scooping him back up. "Oh, it's not a ride kiddo."

"Me turn," he argued.

"Let me have him," Russell held out his arm. "Set him on my lap."

"No. It's okay. You don't…"

"Chels, c'mon."

She pursed her lips before she set Lucas on Russell's lap and Lucas turned to him. He lifted his little hand to his face, and gently rested it on his cheek.

"You have ouchie."

Russell nodded with a smile. "I do have an ouchie. Mommy is making the ouchies go away," he promised him. "Are you ready to ride?"

Lucas nodded and held on to the arms of the chair.

"Okay, Dad. Lucas wants a ride on the ramp."

His father laughed a deep hearty laugh. "Hold on, cowboy." He pushed them both up the ramp and turned them around. "Are you ready?"

"Go," Lucas ordered.

"Hold on tight," Russell whispered in his ear as he wrapped his arm around him.

His father took them down the ramp as slowly as he had the first time and Lucas giggled, which caused everyone to laugh along.

"Again. Again."

"You heard the man, Dad. We need to go again."

And just as any good grandfather would, as if Lucas were his grandson, his father obliged and gave them another ride.

CHELSEA PROMISED herself she wouldn't cry, not until she went to bed, but watching Everett Walker push his son up and down the ramp they'd built for Russell was tugging at her heart. And then when Russell put Lucas on his lap, she had to turn around. It was nearly more than she could handle.

Glenda slipped her arm around Chelsea's waist. "Why don't you go inside and gather yourself. They're going to take him up and down all the ramps, and Lucas seems to be fine right where he is."

She would have protested, but Glenda was right. She needed to gather herself and Lucas didn't need to see her cry.

The moment she walked back into the kitchen, the tears began. Perhaps the scenario would have been different, but in her head, she'd seen Lucas play with Russell and his father many times. Even when he'd written her off, and she'd married someone else, she still had dreamed about him.

The dreams had become more vivid once Dominic was out of the picture. Of course, the moment she'd seen Russell in the hospital—well, she'd dreamed of him every night since.

They were going to be friends. They'd agreed. It broke her heart to think that's all that was left, but it was enough. Above all else, Lucas was happy. That was all that mattered.

She could hear them all move to the garage and Lucas was still laughing.

Chelsea walked into the living room and took a moment in front of the Christmas tree. A new ornament caught her eye, and she reached out to touch it. It said Lucas, and it had a place for a picture of him and Santa, which was left empty.

She covered her mouth as more tears streamed down her cheeks.

Slowly, she turned to the fireplace to see two more stockings had been added on the end next to Russell's. There was one with Lucas's name, and it was next to the stocking with her name which had once hung there many years ago. She pressed her hand to her chest. That was simply one of the best Christmas surprises she'd ever had, and she wasn't even sure Glenda had planned it to be.

Her knees could hardly hold her now. She moved to the nearest seat and fell into it just as Glenda walked into the room carrying two mugs, with tea bags hanging from the sides.

"Let those tears out. Every mama has them."

"Oh, Glenda. I don't know how to accept all of this. Seeing him with Lucas and then the ornament and the stockings," she said as she sobbed. "When it's all over, it's going to break Lucas's heart to leave here—to leave you."

Glenda set the mugs on the coffee table and sat down next to Chelsea. "I believe in fate. They all give me a hard time about it, but I do. I hate to say it, but I think that's what all of this is. It's fate that you're a nursing student, he got hurt, and you needed refuge."

Chelsea chuckled through the tears. "You don't think that's stretching it a bit?"

"No, not at all. So fate made you take a detour, and you got Lucas. You wouldn't give him up would you?"

Her heart sank. "No. Heavens, no."

"See, everything for a reason. Look at Susan and Eric. She was in the cards to cater for me. And Dane and Gia. Well, had he not moved away, Gia would have just been another woman in town, not the woman."

"He doesn't want anything more than friendship from me, and I think that's pushing it. He's cordial, but..."

Glenda patted her hand. "He doesn't know what he wants yet.

I know my son. I saw the way he looked at Lucas when you set him on his lap. That wasn't a look of just friendship, Chelsea. And when he looks at you, well, I've see him look at you like that before, honey."

"What if you're wrong?"

"Well then, I'm wrong. But for now, you're here, and it's Christmas time. We're going to make the best of it."

"I saw the ornament on the tree that says Lucas."

Glenda smiled wide. "He's not afraid of Santa, is he? He'll be dropping by on Christmas Eve."

"You're kidding, right?"

"I don't kid about Christmas. I have that there so when he sits on Santa's lap you'll have a memento."

The tears, which had dried, fell again. "You're too good to us," Chelsea said as she wiped at her cheeks.

"We love you and Lucas. All of us do," she said as she handed Chelsea one of the mugs she'd set on the table.

For the first time in a long time, Chelsea felt that love Glenda talked about. And as she listened carefully, she could hear her son laughing from beyond the back door, and she knew he, too, felt the love they were spoiling them with.

CHAPTER 13

*G*lenda had offered to give Lucas his bath, read him a story, and sit with him until Chelsea was done helping put Russell to bed.

Without protest, Russell had allowed Chelsea to drain his catheter bag, take his vitals, give him his medicines, and even agreed to let her take a warm cloth over his body so that he'd feel refreshed. Though that had been the hardest part of the night, Chelsea thought as she started.

As he sat on the edge of his bed, she removed the sling on his left arm. Carefully she pulled his shirt off of him, and her body temperature began to rise. All she could hope for was that he didn't see the heat rise in her cheeks. This was too familiar, and much too intimate.

Gently she took the cloth over his shoulder and down his arm. For a moment she lingered on the tattoo. It was once a C for Chelsea, but he'd had it added to, and now it was a beautiful, ornate band that encircled his well-formed bicep.

She licked her lips and cleared her mind as she took the cloth across his chest to the other shoulder. Even though his right arm wasn't injured, she took equally as much care to wipe the cloth from his shoulder to his fingers.

His eyes had closed, she noticed, as she worked the cloth around the back of his neck and then over his broad chest and firm stomach. Her breath hitched as she moved in closer to him so that she could reach around him and run the cloth down his muscular back.

She jumped when his hand came to her waist and held her where she was, extremely close to him.

Chelsea looked down at him, and his eyes were wide now looking up at her.

"It's hard to have you this close to me," he said. His voice was full of gravel and heat.

"That's why you should have Karen here full time." Her voice cracked, but she kept her body close, afraid to move.

"That isn't what I meant." His hand slid up her back, and she found she had to rest her hand on his right shoulder to keep her balance. "I'm mad at you. I'm mad down to my core."

"Russ, I'm…"

"You're sorry. You've said that. I'd be fine if you never said it again." She felt the lightness of his fingertips through the fabric of her shirt, and it sent a tingle down the length of her spine. "I lied when I said we should just be friends. I thought I could do it."

Chelsea felt her hand begin to shake. The messages she was getting were mixed. Here he was, holding her close to him, but he didn't want to be friends. She wasn't sure she could go on like this.

Russell lifted his chest and pressed his hand to the center of her back bringing her closer to him still.

"Chelsea, I remember the day I fell in love with you. It was Christmas, too."

She managed a weak breath. "I remember."

"I fell in love tonight, too."

She swallowed hard. "You did?"

"With Lucas."

The tears she'd promised herself for bedtime rushed to the surface and fell just as quickly. "Russ…"

"He's a fantastic kid, Chelsea. I thought it would be hard to see him and know where he came from. But he came from you. And…" His chest expanded as he took a deep breath and locked eyes with her. "And I've never stopped loving you."

Chelsea took her free hand and covered her mouth as the sobbing continued.

"Don't cry," he said as he brushed away the tears on her cheeks.

"Russ, I can't help it. I don't know what to do with it. I don't deserve it."

"My mother would kill me if I said someone didn't deserve a second chance. She thinks like that."

That caused her to chuckle. "She puts a lot of stock in fate."

"Yes, she does." He lifted his hand into her hair. "I hate that I can't stand up and lay you in this bed with me."

"You'll heal quickly. That's how you work."

He gently brushed his thumb over her cheek again. "I'm sorry I accused you."

She stepped back from him and turned to put the cloth away. She couldn't look at him.

"Chelsea?" His voice lost the heat, but she'd noted the panic that had risen in it.

"I should go relieve your mom," she sniffed.

"You should turn around and talk to me. What's going on?"

Chelsea turned to him. "Do you think I would ever want to see you physically hurt? You asking me where I was that night says that you do."

"It was stupid. Chels…"

"It's not stupid. It's honest." This is where truth and feelings always hurt the worst. "That truck was in my garage for the past two years, Russ. The night before you were hit, it was stolen."

His eyes opened wide, and the soft demeanor had vanished. "You didn't mention that."

"I know," she shouted and then turned to close the bedroom door. "I didn't want it. You don't know how many times I'd thought about letting it roll into the lake. So when it was stolen, that was better."

"Until it ran me off the road."

"And showed back up across the street."

"You didn't tell Smythe about this did you?"

She shook her head. "No."

"Call him. Call him right now," he ordered. "I can't tell you why they ran my ass off the road, but that means they were on your property before this all happened."

Chelsea wrung her hands in front of her. "You're not mad at me?"

"Oh, I'm starting to get that way. Chels, you're in danger. Does the ass have a family? A new girlfriend? Some old debt someone's trying to collect on?"

She thought for a moment. "His brother was in jail in Jersey. His mother…" She thought for a moment. "I just never saw her again. She never came back around after they'd kidnapped Lucas."

"They?"

She moved to him and sat on the edge of the bed next to him. "She'd put Dominic up to taking Lucas in the first place. She didn't think I deserved full custody."

"That's not okay. Why wasn't she arrested?"

"She was, on accessory charges. She would have been out by now," she said and the thought scared the hell out of her. "What if she's in contact with Dominc?"

"This is a lot of information. Get my phone. Call Phillip and tell him all of this."

"He's going to have to drive out here, and…"

"He will, too. Just do it. I'm right here by your side," he said taking her hand and giving it a squeeze.

"You always should have been," she admitted, and her gut tightened at the pain of what she'd done to him.

Russell lifted his hand into her hair again and pulled her to him until their lips nearly touched. "I will be now," he promised as he pressed his lips to hers.

The familiarity of it came back as if not a moment had passed between them. She leaned into him and sank into the kiss he offered.

She was careful not to move him too much, but she wanted to feel him—wrap herself around him.

Neither of them heard the door open, nor did they realize anyone was there until Dane cleared his throat.

Chelsea jumped from the bed and wiped her lips.

"Mom never did let us have girls in our rooms. I wonder why," he joked and then looked at Chelsea. "Gia sent this," he said holding up a little box for her. "She brought it back from Lucca for you. She said you'd had your eyes on it."

Chelsea walked to the door and took the wrapped box from him. "I'll save it for Christmas."

"I don't think that was the point," Dane said with a laugh. "Open it."

She slid her finger under the paper and opened the box. Inside was a small snow globe, just like the one she'd seen in Gia's store. It was a Christmas scene, and there was a mom and a little boy looking up at the Christmas tree, and it had reminded her of herself and Lucas.

Another tear escaped and slid down her cheek, which she quickly brushed away. "Thank her for me."

"She'll be here for Christmas. You'll see her then."

She held it to her chest. "I'd better go check on Lucas," she said, and slid past Dane.

. . .

THE LOOK in his brother's eyes said it all.

"You're surprised to see me kissing Chelsea," Russell offered, as he nodded to invite Dane in.

"You could say that. Though, I expected that it would come, in time. We all do."

"Maybe that's why I did it. I'm not sure it's the best thing for me. Not a good time to get involved with her."

"Any other time would be better?"

"When her ex wasn't out on parole and the truck belonging to him hadn't run me off the road. Oh, and when people weren't breaking into her house. Am I missing anything?"

Dane chuckled. "It's messed up, man."

"No kidding. I guess it's a good thing I didn't steal Gia from you then, huh? That would have made this messy."

"Yeah. I'm glad my charms won over. So what do they say about your recovery?"

Russell shrugged. "If I behave and mind my nurse I'll heal faster. Hopefully, they'll let me walk soon and take off all these bandages."

"Good. You look uncomfortable."

"I am. She eases the pain though," he said, and he could feel the lightness of his grin.

"I hope it works out for you. Seems weird that you'd have a kid if you got together."

Russell nodded. "He loves her. She's his world and vice versa."

"And you think there's room for you in that world?"

"I'd like to think so."

Dane pulled his keys from his pocket. "Get some sleep. I'm heading back to town to pick up Gia from the store. They had some Christmas shopping event between all the stores and some vendors in the event center."

"Sounds as if the women are taking over the town."

"It's an awesome sight." Dane gave him a wave and left him alone in the room.

He laid back on the pillows and tucked his right arm under his head.

Dane's words played in his head. Lucas would be his son if things did go in the direction they'd originally planned. He looked at his tattoo, which now bore no resemblance to the C that had once graced it. He supposed if things worked out he'd get a new one. Maybe he could add an L too.

The whole thought made him laugh to himself. Maybe it was just the Florence Nightingale effect. Falling in love with his nurse could just be her taking care of him.

Then again, maybe it was years of anger finally subsiding.

Either way, he'd like to feel it out a little more.

He looked at the nightstand next to him where his phone lay. He picked it up and scrolled through the contacts until he found one that said Officer Smythe.

He pushed the button. "Hey, Phillip. Listen, I think you need to talk to Chelsea. She seems to have forgotten to fill you in on a few things," he said, and then he realized that perhaps he didn't trust her as much as he thought he did. His words and tone were accusatory.

Just as he thought, Phillip said he'd head right out.

Well, this would determine how things went from there.

CHAPTER 14

*G*lenda had bathed Lucas and put him to bed. Everett had pushed the bed to the wall and made sure Lucas wouldn't fall out.

Chelsea readied herself for bed, slipping into an old tank top and shorts, then tied her hair in a ponytail atop her head.

She heard Glenda quietly call her name from beyond the door, and then tap softly.

Chelsea walked to the door and pulled it open.

"I'm sorry to bother you. Officer Smythe is here and wants to talk to you. I can sit with Lucas."

She could feel the heat crawl up her skin. He'd called him after she left, she realized. They should have done that together.

Ensuring that a smile came to her lips, she nodded. "I'll be right down. Let me put on a robe."

Russell and Phillip Smythe were in the living room when she walked in. Russell had managed to get a shirt on, whether he did that alone or not, she wasn't sure. Phillip was in a faded pair of jeans and a T-shirt. His coat was draped over the edge of the sofa. This couldn't even wait until he was on duty, she observed.

"It's past ten o'clock," she noted the time aloud wondering if they were aware, because a mother of a young son certainly was.

Phillip stood from his seat. "I'm sorry to come so late. But when Russ called, I thought it was urgent enough to make the drive."

She shifted a glance to Russell, and it apparently relayed her feelings as he shifted in his chair.

"Chels, he needs to know what you know."

Phillip moved to her and touched her arm. "I need all the details, so I know what's going on. We have two cases here, and they're tying together, and you're in the middle of them. You can't hold anything back from me. I don't want to have to arrest you."

She sucked in a hard breath. "You'd arrest me?"

"I have reason to suspect that you ran Russell off the road," he said as he removed his hand from her arm.

Chelsea turned to Russell. "Is that what you told him you thought? You think I did this? Even when I told you I didn't?"

Russell took a breath to speak, but Phillip moved between them. "No, that's not what he said. In fact, all he told me was you had some information that I might like to know."

She bit down on her lip. "Fine."

Phillip stepped back and motioned for her to sit down. "Tell me about the truck."

She adjusted the robe around her and sat down on the sofa. "The truck had been parked in my garage for the past two years. It was stolen the day before Russell was hit."

"That's burglary. You didn't think to mention it?" Phillip's tone stayed even, but it stabbed at her all the same.

"Listen, I would have dumped the truck if I could. I didn't want it around. I hated it."

"So someone has been on your property numerous times?"

"I guess so."

She saw the color change of expression on Phillip's face. Her answers were only feeding into his anger with her.

"You guess so. Chels, this is serious. Do you realize that with this information now I can arrest you on suspicion?" Phillip's voice rose.

She gasped in response and Russell leaned in. "That's not necessary, is it? I mean we both know she didn't do it."

"Do we?" Phillip stood. "Who else knew that truck was in your garage?"

She shrugged. "Anyone Dominic might have told it was there."

"He's been questioned about this already. About his connection to the truck and the accident. He said he left the truck for his brother."

"Who is in jail," she offered.

"Confirmed."

Russell shook his head. "Sweet little family you married into," he quipped, which forced her to her feet.

"What about you? What did you do to cause someone to want to run your ass off the road? Were you just sitting quietly in the bar minding your own business? No. Russell Walker was in an argument with someone."

"You're going to stand over me and pick a fight?"

"That's what you do best. Not me."

"No, you just walk away from them."

Anger pulsed through her, and she had all intentions of walking away from this one too until Phillip took her by the shoulders.

"Sit down, and both of you cool it."

Chelsea did as she was told, but not without reservation.

Phillip sat down and clasped his hands, resting his arms on his knees. "One thing we know. These items are related, we just need to find out why and how." He turned to Chelsea. "What else didn't you tell me?"

She shook her head. "That was all. I just wanted that truck gone, and it was. I'm sorry."

"You haven't had any connection to his family at all?"

"Phillip, he kidnapped my son and his mother was in on it. Do you think I'd stay in touch?"

Phillip shook his head. "I have to ask, Chels."

Russell tapped his fingers on the arm of his chair. "You don't think it could just be random? I mean, it would be weird, but maybe?"

"Maybe," Phillip said. "I'm going back out tomorrow to talk to the bartender on duty the night they ran you down. She's been gone the past week."

"Lila." He said, and Chelsea shot him a heated look.

"You know her name?" she asked, through gritted teeth.

"Yep," he said with a knowing nod. "Thought I was going to get lucky that night, so I remembered it. Who knew, huh?" he snapped out his answer so that it would do maximum damage.

Phillip stood. "You two might just be one another's demise," he said shaking his head. "Tomorrow is Christmas Eve. Why don't you find some spirit? I'll be in touch," he informed them as he walked out of the room and they heard the door close behind him.

Chelsea wrapped her arms around herself. "I'll help you back into bed," she offered without looking at him.

"I wish I could tell you I'd do it my damn self. I hate having to rely on you."

"I'm beginning not to like it too much either," she quipped.

"You liked it just fine an hour ago when you were pressing your body against mine."

That caused her to turn. "You lured me in."

"You wanted me to."

"So you did that for me?"

"Ye..." he stopped, and she watched as he processed his answer. The color in his cheeks began to fade, and he looked up at her with sad eyes. "No. I didn't do that for you," he said. His voice drifted off. "I've missed you so much it hurt. For a moment I had you in my arms, and everything seemed right again."

Chelsea shifted her weight from foot to foot, still hugging herself as if it were her only comfort. "It did seem right."

"Why do we do this?"

"We want to hurt each other."

"Well, I don't like to be hurt."

She knew that meant a lot of things, but nothing would stop her from taking it personally. "I don't like it either."

"I'll take your help getting into bed, but will you spend a few moments with me?" he asked as he rolled his chair toward her.

"Your mom is sitting with Lucas."

"Just a few minutes," he said reaching his hand out to her.

"Okay."

AS THEY WALKED BACK to his room, and she pushed him through the doorway, Russell thought back to when they were together, planning a life. Things were volatile then, too. Arguments were often and furious. The makeup sex was good, though. The very thought brought a smile to his face.

"What are you grinning about?" she asked as she stopped pushing his chair and locked the wheels.

He looked up and noticed she was looking at him in the dresser mirror. "Honestly, I was thinking of how many fights we've had like this. But we used to fix it with makeup sex."

Chelsea's cheeks colored pink, and she shook her head. "Those are better memories."

She fixed his bed, pulling down the sheets and fluffing up the pillows.

As she did so, he watched her. He knew that body, hidden under the robe. He was painfully aware that they wouldn't be having makeup sex after their fight. In fact, they hadn't made very good strides into, well, whatever it was they were heading into. But he wondered just how far he could take it before she'd smack him.

When Chelsea bent over, he reached out his hand and laid it on her rear, giving it a gentle squeeze. If he were right, she'd fly up at him, and it would be over.

Instead, she gently turned her head and narrowed her eyes on him. "Seriously?"

"Can't blame a guy from trying, right?"

She turned slowly and faced him. Pulling at the tie on the robe, she let it fall open and to the floor.

Russell let out a chuckle when he saw the tank top and shorts underneath. "Wasn't what I was expecting," he joked.

"Yeah, as if I'd answer the call of the police naked under my robe."

"Every man has a fantasy."

She stepped toward him. "You're sure you want to go down this road?" she asked, inching in and leaning her hands on the arms of his chair. "This is one grand mess we've gotten ourselves into. It's Christmas. I'm in hiding with my son. You're in a wheelchair. We haven't spoken in three years. It's obvious we only pick fights with each other."

"Doesn't mean I don't want to cop a feel." He winked, and she stepped back, but he caught her wrist. "Yes, I'm sure I want to go down this road. I can't think of a nicer Christmas present."

Her eyes went soft, and she moved into him now, balancing against his chair, and kissed him deeply. Yeah, that's what he'd been looking for, he thought, as he let his hand slide up under the back of her shirt and she moaned against him.

She let her hand glide up his neck and into his hair, and he thought he might just have the strength to lift himself from that chair to hold her.

With a ragged breath, he eased back. "This is frustrating."

"It won't be long."

"Do you think we can stay civil until we can...do this?" He nodded his head toward his bed.

"It's not about sex, right?"

Of course, she'd ask that. And really, why shouldn't she? "No. Let's just say, if my big fat mouth got me this opportunity again, I'm going to try to make the most of it...and not let my big fat mouth lose it for me."

She tucked a strand of blonde hair, which had fallen from the knot atop her head, behind her ear. Her lips were pink and swollen now, so when she smiled it made everything inside him come alive.

"I've missed you, Russ. From the moment I made my very bad decision—I've missed you. I'd give anything for another chance."

He reached for her hand and gave it a squeeze. "Okay, then. Let's make the best of this."

CHAPTER 15

*I*t was Karen that greeted Russell the next morning and wasn't that a disappointment. Again, she checked him out, washed him up, and this time, she did some physical therapy which hurt like a son-of-a-bitch.

"You're strong. I think that most of the estimates they have of you getting back on your feet are inaccurate. You'll be up in no time."

"Good. I'm done with this."

"Ah, where's your Christmas spirit?" she asked, just as his Christmas toddled in the door.

He looked up to see Lucas walking in with a sports bottle of water and smiling as Chelsea followed.

"Dwink," Lucas said as he handed the bottle to Russell.

"Thanks, pal." He took the bottle and then ran his hand over Lucas's soft hair. He wasn't sure what had driven him to do it, but the sheer pleasure of it sent a jolt right through him.

"Miss Quinn, why don't you get your notes on your patient and let's look at them."

Chelsea nodded. "They're in my room. I'll be right back. C'mon, Lucas."

"He's fine right here," Russell offered, again, not sure why, but there was great pleasure in having him there.

Chelsea nodded and left the room.

"He's not bothering you during your rehabilitation is he?" Karen asked as Lucas walked to the window and looked outside.

"No. He seems to be equally as good a nurse as his mother is," he said.

"Sometimes children are the best medicine. You need to let her know if that changes, though," she said, her brows raised as if to make a point.

"I will."

Chelsea returned with her notes and with Russell's mother, who took Lucas to do something else. He listened as the women discussed him, right in front of him, and he focused in on Chelsea's voice as she answered every question Karen had for her. She was brilliant, he thought. Every patient that had her for a nurse would be well taken care of.

Karen gave her instructions, which Chelsea jotted down. They discussed his pending doctor's appointment for the day after Christmas. When Karen packed up to leave, she leaned into him. "Have a nice Christmas. I'll see you in a few days. Esther will be here tomorrow."

"Chelsea can't just take care of me?"

"Not yet, but she's doing a great job," she said, and Russell shifted his gaze to Chelsea, who was still writing down notes in her notebook.

"I think she is, too," he offered, and Karen smiled.

It was nearly lunchtime when Russell's father came for him. "I told your mother I was taking you to check fences. I've already gotten some feedback on that not being good for you. So if I catch hell taking you into town…"

"We'll be okay, Dad. Hey, I sent an email to that prefabricated housing company and set us up an appointment in January."

His father laughed as he unlocked the wheels to the wheelchair and began to push Russell from the bedroom. "You're serious about all of this, huh?" he asked as he pushed him out to the driveway.

"Time to think about settling down I think."

His father opened the door to his mother's car, which was easier for him to slide into than his father's truck.

"Settle down? That sounds like wife and kids talk."

"Maybe," he offered, as his father helped lift him from the chair and ease him into the car.

Once he was settled, his father put the wheelchair in the trunk, and then climbed in next to him.

"Back to this settling in. Does this have something to do with Chelsea?"

Russell laughed. "Maybe."

"Do you think that's a good idea? Things are a bit unstable right now with everything going on in her life and with you suffering these injuries."

"Mom says it's fate."

His father let out a snort of disapproval as he turned onto the dirt road that would lead them into town.

"Your mom buys into fate much more than I do. I just don't want to see you get hurt. If Phillip Smythe is right, and it was her husband's truck that ran you off the road…"

"Ex-husband."

"Whatever," his father said lifting his hands from the wheel for emphasis. "Some connection with her nearly got you killed. As your father, a lifetime commitment to this sounds a little crazy. Especially since you're talking about it while you're still ankle to groin in a huge bandage and a wheelchair, and she's hiding out in our house."

There was validity to his father's worries, but at the moment he wasn't going to think about it. He was going to focus on going Christmas shopping and getting home before anyone noticed they'd been missing for hours.

As they merged onto the main road, Russell could feel the tension build in his body. They'd be passing the guardrail he went through. He braced for it as they came up on it.

"Slow down, would you. I want to see this," he said to his father, who did as he asked and actually pulled to the shoulder.

"I usually drive the other way. I didn't want your mother to see this," he admitted.

Russell looked at the road ahead where his tire tracks still stained the pavement. The railing was taped off, but his truck had done quite a job on them before they gave way and his truck flipped down the hill and into the trees.

He held his breath. Nearly two weeks later and it still looked horrible. Closing his eyes, he tried to remember anything he could about that night.

Innocently, he'd gone to the bar to let off a little steam. He'd been worked up over his brother going to Italy with Gia. It had been stupid, but he was lonely, and when things hadn't worked out for himself with Gia, well, he just wanted a night to forget.

He'd had all of two beers before he'd begun making moves on the bartender. Yes, he'd gotten into it with someone who didn't care much for the Walkers, though he hadn't offered up much reasoning, except to say Byron Walker had once screwed him out of a job or something. It hadn't been much of a surprise, as many people didn't care for Russell's uncle. It was when he'd made a comment about his father that Russell remembered getting mad, but even then he'd let the comment slide. And then the man said something about not being man enough for Chelsea. That had struck a chord. He'd made it a point to bring up the knowledge that she had to get some on the side and challenged his manhood again. That's when he got in the man's face.

They never hit each other. Only words had been exchanged, but they were heated.

There was a woman there, too. She'd been older, and he remembered looking at her thinking that she must have had a hell of a life, and it showed like a map on her face. Her skin was pale, and her hair nearly black. It was a stark contrast.

She had held off the man, telling him that Russell wasn't worth the energy, but he didn't remember them following him to his truck that night. All he remembered was finishing his beer, tipping the bartender, and leaving.

"You doing okay?" his father asked, and Russell realized he'd closed his eyes.

"Yeah. I was just trying to remember being run off the road."

"And?"

"I don't."

"We'd better finish our shopping. Where do you want to go first?"

WITH RUSSELL OUT WITH EVERETT, Chelsea found it nice just to relax for a few hours. Lydia had dropped by with baked goods for Glenda for Christmas, and she stayed to chat with Chelsea.

They sat on the back porch of the Walker house. Chelsea had a jacket wrapped around her to keep her warm, and a cup of tea between her hands. Lucas was blowing bubbles in the cold, which Lydia had brought over for him. She would never have imagined this was how they would spend Christmas Eve.

"I drove by your house this morning on my way back from the event center. Smythe was loading things into his truck."

"I asked him to get Lucas's bed, a gate, and his highchair. They were things we didn't think of the first time, but it'll make it easier here."

"I'm sure between all of Russell's brothers and cousins, you could have had them move them for you. Why ask Smythe?" she growled.

"He offered, and he checks up on the house. It's his opportunity to see if it's been compromised again."

"You, my friend, are living many different hells. Your ex is on parole. Your house is broken into, and you're forced out of it. And you have to spend all this extra time with Smythe. He's never been a fan of the Walkers, you know."

Chelsea shook her head. "No," she whispered. "He's never been a fan of Byron Walker because he causes trouble," she reminded her.

Lydia nodded in agreement. "He's certainly had a lot of work because of him. And Jake's street racing hasn't helped his attitude toward the Walkers."

Chelsea laughed. "I think he's learned his lesson there."

Lydia sat back in her chair and warmed her hands on her mug. "How does Russ do with Lucas? That's been a sore spot for him, you know."

"I can imagine. He wasn't ready to accept him, but I think he might have fallen in love."

"With Lucas?"

Chelsea nodded, as she watched him spin in circles. "I think they'll be good for each other."

Lydia leaned in, her arms on her legs. "Are you sure about this? Do you really want to go back there?"

"It was a good place to be, Lydia. I messed it up."

"You fight a lot."

That made her chuckle. "We still do. But if he'll give me another chance, I won't turn it down."

"Do you think it's your ex that tried to hurt him?"

She shook her head. "I think it's coincidence."

"You believe that just randomly, whoever stole that truck decided to run him off the road?"

"I have to believe that. I can't think that this is my fault at all. I wasn't there. And it's only chance that I happened to be on that floor at the hospital for rotation when he came in. This is life offering me a second chance," she assured her friend.

Lydia relaxed back. "We're a mess, you know? You love a man with a temper and a mouth that causes people to run him off of roads. And the only man who is interested in me is the one man I have no interest in."

"Are you sure?"

"The only thing I'm more sure about is that I'd rather die alone than to give in to him," she said with a curt nod.

Chelsea turned when she heard the door behind them slide open. She nearly laughed when Phillip Smythe walked through it.

Lydia gripped her mug tighter and her lips pursed.

"Afternoon, Ladies," he said lightheartedly.

"Good afternoon," Chelsea greeted, but Lydia kept her eyes forward.

"Chels, the things I brought from your house are in the garage. Mrs. Walker thought that would work for now. She'll have Gerald and Ben bring them up for you. I also brought those other items I'd been holding," he said, as he looked at Lucas.

"I appreciate it. Can I get you some coffee or tea?" she offered and noticed Lydia shift her a steel-eyed look.

"I have to get back to town. I'm going back over the tapes from the bar."

"Do you think you'll find something."

"I hope so," he said. "I'd like to give Russ some closure."

"He'd appreciate that."

"Where is he?" Phillip asked, but she noticed his eyes had diverted to Lydia, who kept her attention directed away.

"He went out with Everett to check the fences. They've been gone for a very long time, though."

"Perhaps they stopped up at Eric's."

"That could be," she agreed. She hadn't thought of that.

"I'll leave you two to your drinks." He turned to leave and stopped again. "Goodbye, Lydia."

Lydia huffed out a breath. "Bye," she said sarcastically, without ever looking over her shoulder.

Phillip smiled and headed back into the house.

Lucas jumped around the yard a bit more. His little nose had become cherry red, and Chelsea's tea had gone cold. As she stood to gather up her son, the door opened again, and Russell poised his chair at the top of the ramp.

Lucas looked up and with an enormous smile on his little lips. He ran toward him. "Ride."

The smile on Russell's face matched that of her son's, and she felt her heart swell in her chest.

"Dad, you heard him," Russell said, and Everett picked up Lucas, set him on Russell's lap, and pushed them down the ramp to the patio where she sat with Lydia. "It's chilly out here," he said as Lucas snuggled up to him and rested his head against him.

"He's been a little cooped up in the house. I thought it was good to let him run," she said as she gazed at the two of them together.

"I should head back home," Lydia stood. "My grandfather is trying to make nice by having dinner tonight. It should be interesting."

Lydia kissed Chelsea on the cheek and then did the same for both Russell and Lucas before she walked through the house.

When Chelsea turned back, she noticed Lucas had already fallen asleep on Russell's lap, and Russell was gazing at him, much as she did, herself, when he'd sleep. He brushed his hand over his head, his fingers lingering on his forehead. She thought she might cry at the sight.

"Did Mom tell you Santa is coming to visit him tonight?"

"She did. She's gone above and beyond."

"She loves Christmas. She put stockings up for you both too."

"I saw them. She's made me feel like part of the family."

Russell reached his hand out to her, and she took it. "You are part of this family. So is he."

She squeezed his hand. "That was all I ever wanted, Russ. You have to know that."

"I do now." He shifted slightly so he could reach into his pocket, under Lucas's body. "So I have a confession. Dad and I weren't out checking fencelines."

"You shouldn't leave the house," she scolded.

"I know. But I wanted to go to town and do some shopping."

Chelsea narrowed her eyes on him. "Karen had better not find out."

He laughed. "She won't. I wanted to get something for you, and I can't wait until tomorrow to give it to you." He handed her a small wrapped box, and now the tears did come.

"Russ..."

"Go on," he said as he wrapped his arm around Lucas and held him close.

Between the thoughtfulness of the gift in her hands and the sight in front of her, she thought perhaps her heart might melt.

She unwrapped the box and pulled it open to reveal a diamond, heart-shaped pendant. She pulled out the necklace and held it up.

"Oh, Russell. This is too much."

"You have a beautiful heart, Chels. I wanted to commemorate it. I think becoming a nurse fits you. You've always cared for people, and the two of us know how much you give to others, first hand," he said before he placed a kiss on Lucas's head.

Chelsea covered her mouth with her hand. "It's beautiful."

"Put it on. I'm not much help right now," he joked.

Chelsea unclasped the hook, slipped it around her neck, and rehooked it. "Well?"

"It pales in your beauty," he complimented softly.

"It's moments like this that I think we'll never fight again."

"Don't count on it." He took her hand and pulled her closer to him. "I'm not going to let you go this time. This time, I'll fight for you. For both of you."

"That's a big promise."

"Yeah, well my eyes are open now. I love both of you, and that's a lot coming from me. I can't see ever letting either of you leave me."

Chelsea held her hand over her heart. "Russell, you've been around him for a few days. What if you find out that it's too much? You and I, we've loved each other before. We know what to expect. Things are different now. Can you really look at him every day and not be reminded of what I did to break your heart?"

"I look at my mother and how she looks at Eric. He wasn't easy on her. And he was eight when our dad married her. Chels, if she can love Eric as much as she does, I know that in my heart I can love Lucas for who he is, and not think about his genetics. Family can be chosen too."

"I love you, Russell Walker. You need to know that no matter what I've ever done, I never stopped loving you."

He pulled her in closer until their lips met. And though it was a simple kiss, it held so much promise.

Lucas squirmed beneath them, and she backed away. "I should go put him down for a nap."

"Why don't you put him in my room, we'll be near enough for him then."

She nodded and scooped up her son as she stood. And as she carried him into the house, she kissed him softly on the cheek. He already smelled of Russell.

As she lay him down on Russell's bed, she looked down at his fair skin, and his white-blond hair. There had never been a more perfect human conceived, she thought. Russell saw that in him too. She knew that to be true. Maybe they could have it all and Russell could love them both. Wouldn't that make it the best Christmas ever?

CHAPTER 16

Keeping Lucas out of the presents was a full-time job for everyone who had gathered for dinner. Russell knew his father was a patient man, but until he'd picked up Lucas for the tenth time to distract him, he hadn't quite understood how patient he was. It didn't seem to weigh on him, this child that just happened into their lives and was disrupting everything around them—in a good way.

It was killing Russell to sit and watch everyone moving about, setting the table, pouring drinks, just being normal. Susan was fussing with some dish, while Chelsea tended to the pumpkin pie she'd promised Gerald she'd make. Somehow, Russell managed to get himself in a corner, and the world moved on without him—until she came to him.

Pearl had dropped by a dress from her bridal store for Chelsea to wear tonight. It was a bridesmaid sample and more of a party dress than a wedding dress. It fit her like a glove. She'd curled her hair, and golden strands cascaded down over her bare shoulders. She was as lovely as he'd ever remembered her.

"I brought you a drink," she said, handing him a wine glass.

He sniffed the liquid inside. "This is grape juice."

She smiled. "Can't mix drugs and alcohol," she joked, and he humored her with a laugh. Karen had made it a fact to remind him more than once that he could do his celebrating after the holidays.

"Come here," he said, motioning her toward him. "Sit down."

"There is nowhere to sit."

"I want you on my lap, so you're close to me."

She moved in closer. "I don't want to hurt you."

"You won't. You know where all of my no-no places are," he joked, and she laughed as she carefully eased herself down on his lap with her body mostly on his good leg and the chair. It would have to do, he thought. But in a month, he was going to sweep her up in his arms and carry her away. They'd dance, too, when he could walk again. There was a lot of healing to be done, he decided.

"This is nice." Chelsea nuzzled her nose in the crease of his neck, and he breathed in sharply at the sensations it sent through him.

"Maybe this was more dangerous than I thought," he whispered. "I'm still a warm-blooded man, and I can't do anything about this," he growled low.

"Mom's ready," Dane shouted toward them. "Get to the table before Dad eats all the turkey."

They both laughed, and Chelsea placed a gentle kiss on his lips before he stood. "We can't keep your mom waiting."

No, he knew that was a bad idea anytime.

CHRISTMAS MUSIC PLAYED while the entire Walker family ate dinner around the table. It had changed a bit, Chelsea noted, as she looked around. Once, she'd eaten among them all, and she was the only girlfriend there. Now Eric sat next to his wife, Susan. Dane sat next to his fiancée Gia. Ben and Gerald took their positions on each side of Everett at the end of the extended table.

But really, the big difference was that she was back at this same table, years later. Her seat was next to Russell's as it always had been, and Lucas, in his highchair, was between them—as if they were a family.

The thought caught in her chest, and she swallowed hard. Her fingers itched to touch the necklace at her throat, but she didn't want to draw attention to it. It held a bit of a secret—Russell had gone to town to get it. Glenda would be furious.

Lucas had seen the many wrapped gifts under the tree, and he was old enough to understand that he wanted to unwrap them.

Chelsea did her best to keep him seated in his chair.

"It's no wonder you're so skinny," Glenda said to her as she tried to help Lucas with his dinner. "You don't eat. He'll be fine. It'll make it to his mouth or on the floor. You need to eat too."

"Oh, I'd rather help him than mess up your nice carpet."

Glenda leaned in toward her over the table. "Sweetheart, this house has seen my five young boys run through it, and two more before them, when their father and his brother were children. One more isn't going to hurt it. And I'll tell you what. He's already making my Christmas brighter, so he couldn't possibly make a mess big enough to take that away from me."

She caught Russell's stare, and it brought a warmth to her. Yes, she'd taken a turn from this family—from Russell—but fate had brought her back here. This was where she belonged.

The doorbell diverted everyone's attention from the meal, and Glenda's eyes grew wide. "Lucas, do you want to go with me and see who's at the door?"

Eager to jump down from his chair, Lucas nodded and reached for his mother.

Chelsea quickly cleaned him off and pulled him from the chair. He raced around the table to take Glenda's hand, and together they hurried to the door.

"I need to get my phone and take some pictures," she said as she too hurried around Russell and the table.

She could hear the jingle of bells, a mighty "Ho-ho-ho", and then the joyous squeal of her son's voice all before she got to where they stood.

Lucas jumped up and down, still gripping tightly to Glenda's hand. Chelsea took a picture and then looked at Santa, who smiled widely. Those were familiar eyes beyond that beard. Was there nothing Officer Phillip Smythe wouldn't do for her and her son? The thought made her chuckle. What would Lydia think of her nemesis now?

"Merry Christmas, Lucas," Santa said, and Lucas's eyes went wide. "Can you help me with my bag?"

Lucas nodded, and with one hand still gripping tightly to Glenda's, he wrapped his other hand around Santa's bag and helped him drag it into the living room.

Chelsea could hear the others chuckle, and she hoped they wouldn't give away the identity of Santa.

"You're strong," Santa said to Lucas. "Now, where can I sit so that I can visit with my little friend?"

"Santa, I have a chair all ready for you," Glenda said gesturing to the chair next to the tree.

"Oh, that looks like a good chair." Santa dragged his bag toward the tree, and Lucas followed. "Would you like to sit with me, Lucas?"

Lucas shifted a look to Glenda and then to Chelsea. Each of them nodded their encouragement.

He slowly took a step toward Santa, then took the hand he offered, and Santa hoisted him on his lap.

Chelsea was so caught up in the moment Glenda had to remind her to take the picture.

She lifted her phone, zoomed in the camera, and had to take a very deep breath. The smile on her son's face was one she'd never seen before. That thrill and wonder of childhood was lit in his eyes. She'd feared from the moment he was born that Lucas wouldn't know these kinds of joys, but she'd been wrong. He was seated on Santa's lap and the whole world was right with him.

Chelsea took the picture and lowered her phone, only to realize that Russell was next to her now, reaching up to take her hand.

"Who knew he could be such a convincing Santa?" he whispered.

"He's perfect."

"I'm glad you're both here, Chels," he said, and she looked down at him. "I would have hated to have missed this moment in his life."

Her lips twitched as the tears began to pool in her eyes.

Russell gave her hand a tug and pulled her down to his lap. "I love you both," he whispered in her ear. "I can't believe it took this to tell you that."

"We love you. All of you," she whispered back, resting her head against his. "I only wish his story had started here," she admitted.

"It's just starting, Chels. And so is our story." He wrapped his arm around her and gave her a squeeze.

"Ho-ho-ho, I think I have something in my bag for you." Santa looked at Lucas. "Do you like presents?"

Again he looked at Chelsea for approval, and she nodded.

Lucas nodded to Santa.

"I'm going to need your help to pull it out, okay?" Lucas nodded again and jumped down from Santa's lap. "Reach inside, Lucas. Can you feel another bag?" Lucas nodded. "Pull that out."

Lucas pulled as hard as he could, and then Ben got on his knees next to him. "You want some help?"

"Yes," Lucas said with determination.

Ben grinned as he and Lucas pulled the bag from Santa's bag. This bag had a bright red bow and pictures of Santa all over it.

Ben found the end to the bow and pointed it out to Lucas. "Give this a pull," he said.

Lucas pulled the ribbon, and the bag fell open around a brand new tricycle with police stickers and red and blue lights.

He hurried to get it out of the captive bag, with Ben's help. And as soon as it was free, he climbed on.

Chelsea hurried to her feet to stop him, but both Glenda and Everett held up their hands to let her know he was free to drive it in their house. Truly they were kind people.

"Lucas, there's a siren too," Santa told him, his voice still deep to keep in character.

Lucas looked for the switch and quickly enough found it. He took his first lap from the living room, down the hall, through the kitchen, into the dining room, and back to a full room of people who cheered for him.

Quickly, Chelsea's happy tears turned into a sob. She could never have given him a Christmas like this.

Santa stood and walked to her. He gave her a big hug, and she laughed through the tears as his squishy fat belly pressed against her.

"Merry Christmas, Chelsea," he said softly.

"Merry Christmas, Santa." She kissed him on his cheek. "I don't know when, but I'll pay for that tricycle. That's too much."

He shook his head. "He has a lot of friends in the police department who made that very special bag happen. There are a few more little things in there. We've got his back, and yours."

The tears continued, and Russell guided her back to his lap. He pressed a finger to the necklace he'd given her. "See, your heart feeds others. Your kindness leads the way, sweetheart."

She wished she could look in his eyes and hear the words he spoke, and believe them. She'd hurt him so badly, what made him want to have her there, with her son, and love her as he was? This was the Russell Walker she'd known. This side of him that balanced out the hot-tempered one. She loved him. She'd always loved him.

"I'll make it all right for you, Russell. I'll make it all up. All the wrongs and all the missed opportunities. All of this," she said acknowledging the room of people still cheering her son as he made yet another circle through the rooms.

"We have a lifetime to make up for three lost years. I think we can wash them under the bridge."

He reached his hand up into her hair and pulled her close to him. Pressing his lips to her, she felt his promise. Through this tragedy, they had been given another chance and she sure as hell wasn't going to ruin it.

CHAPTER 17

*L*ucas had worn himself out. He'd ridden his new tricycle until he'd fallen asleep on the handlebars.

Gerald had then picked him up and laid him on the sofa with a stuffed bear, which Santa had also brought him.

Each of Russell's brothers kissed their mother goodnight and then did the same to Chelsea. Gerald lingered and whispered, "I'm glad you're back."

Her heart was full, and she hadn't expected that. The moment Phillip had told her that her ex was out on parole, her house had been broken into, and Russell Walker's name was on her hospital board, she'd expected only horrible things to happen. Who knew, at such a time, it could go so right.

Everett walked into the kitchen when the last of the dishes were being loaded into the dishwasher. "Lucas's bed is all set up for him, and the gate is in the doorway."

"Thank you." Chelsea moved to him and kissed his cheek. "I should go get him upstairs and get him tucked in."

"Oh, well, I took some liberties." He exchanged glances with Glenda, who smiled. "His bed is in Russell's room."

Chelsea felt her mouth drop open. "I don't know if that's…"

Glenda moved in and touched her arm. "I had him bring your things down too." She moved in closer and whispered, "He's better when you're both closer. It's time you be a family."

Chelsea was sure she'd nearly stopped breathing. They may have once been inseparable, and destined to be together, but that was many years ago. Could that really be repaired in a few weeks?

She turned to Russell whose warm smile answered that question very simply.

"Bonus for me. My parents condone a girl sleeping in my room."

She could feel the heat fill her cheeks. "Thank you," was all she could say.

Chelsea scooped Lucas up off the sofa. He stirred awake and made sure he had his bear with him. Then, he caught sight of Russell and reached for him.

Russell lifted his arm, and Chelsea set him on Russell's lap. Lucas looked up at him with sleepy eyes. "You tuck," he said as he rested his head against Russell's chest.

Chelsea watched as Glenda had to turn away and wipe the tear from her cheek. She wasn't so sure Russell hadn't done the same.

She got behind his chair and pushed *their* family into the bedroom to tuck in for the night.

RUSSELL WASN'T USUALLY the kind of man who let his emotions get the best of him. But the moment Lucas had reached for him, he realized he'd become a complete softy.

He loved this little boy as he much as he loved his mother. Russell kissed the top of his head as Chelsea lifted him from his lap.

Lucas woke in protest. "Dad tuck."

Chelsea's hand went straight to her mouth and nearly covered the sob. Her eyes moved to his, but he couldn't read her. Were those happy or sad tears?

"His name is…" she began, and Russell lifted his hand to stop her.

"Let's talk about this alone," he whispered. "Lucas, let your mommy put on your pajamas. I'll kiss you and Bear goodnight, and I'll try to tuck you in. Okay?"

Lucas nodded slightly, climbed out of Russell's chair, and went to Chelsea.

She set him on his little bed and began pulling off his clothes as his body swayed back and forth, since he was still mostly asleep.

"Mommy loves you," she cooed and kissed him on the cheek.

"Wuv you," he said as he cuddled the bear and laid on his pillow. Then, as if he'd received a jolt of energy, he sat up and reached for Russell.

"He can't get out of his chair yet, Lucas," Chelsea told him.

Lucas's little forehead crinkled in thought. He climbed from the bed and went to Russell. In a quick move, and with Russell helping with his good arm, he climbed into the chair and wrapped his arms around Russell's neck. "Wuv you, Daddy." He kissed Russell's cheek and climbed back down.

Without hesitation, he climbed into his bed and was immediately back to sleep.

Both Russell and Chelsea sat there silently, staring at him. If he could stand from that stupid chair, he'd walk outside in the cold and collect himself. The child, whom he'd feared seeing, had completely disarmed him by calling him Daddy.

Chelsea stood and walked to the bathroom. She turned on the light, then turned off the light in the bedroom. He watched as she stood there collecting herself, then he scooted the chair to the door with his foot.

"Don't be angry. He doesn't know who I am," Russell whispered.

Her damp eyes went wide, and her nostrils flared. She was mad. He'd seen this side enough times to know.

She stepped back and motioned to him to get in the bathroom with her. When he managed, she shut the door.

"Angry? You think I'm angry?" she whispered loudly.

"You don't want him to call me dad. It upset you."

"No." The word came on a sob. "It surprised me. It moved me."

He reached out his hand to her. "It moved me too."

"I don't want to confuse him."

Russell let out a long breath. "You plan to let his father be part of his life, then?"

She shook her head. "No. By law, he has been removed from his life. He has no rights to him."

"But Lucas knows his father?'

"No."

"Then what's to confuse him?"

She turned from him and then spun back. "He just met you. The kids at the daycare have dads. He knows about them, he just never..."

"Never realized he didn't have one around?" She nodded. "Are you opposed to me being his dad?"

She lifted her eyes to meet his. "It's all I ever wanted. He should have been your son."

"Then let him be."

"Russell, you're not one to take on someone else's kid."

"Says who?"

She opened her mouth to argue, but then closed it again. "That's a lot of responsibility. It's not just giving him rides on your lap in your wheelchair. It's not just friends showing up as Santa. There's so much more to it."

"Have you met my family? Have you met my father? Chelsea, I'm not a stranger to what it takes."

"He'd be lucky to have a man like your father."

"I'd be honored to try and be like my father."

"And when you get out of that chair, then what? When my duty ends here, then what? Russell, this is all new."

"No. It's just been on hiatus. Let me be his father. Let him call me Dad. I want the job. I'm begging for the job."

"You've been around him a few days. This is a lifetime you're talking about."

"And if he had been my son, I'd still have loved him in those first few days and taken it on for a lifetime."

Chelsea leaned against the counter. "I want perfect for him, Russ. I don't just want names to change. If you're only going to be Russell to him, then be that."

He smiled, and he could see the line between her brows form in confusion. "You don't want me just to be Russell and have him call me dad. Daddies and mommies go together."

She chuckled. "Yes, I guess that's what I'm saying."

"Marry me tomorrow then. Make this a Christmas no one will ever forget."

Chelsea let out a breath of annoyance and tossed her hands in the air. "Don't just throw that around, Russell. That's not funny."

"I'm not laughing."

She moved to him and knelt down in front of him. "As perfect as it sounds, it's impractical."

He shook his head and laughed. "It sounds that way. Marry me anyway, Chelsea. Marry me and let me adopt Lucas. Let me be his daddy. Let my parents be his grandparents. I'm sure you can tell, no one is going to turn him away."

She took his hand in hers and kissed his knuckles. "I need something from you first. I need you to look me in the eye and tell me you forgive me. I have yet to forgive myself, but if you..."

"I forgive you, Chels. I forgive you for being human and making a decision that turned out in some ways to be a blessing. I forgive you for breaking my heart, for the moment, and teaching me that nothing is forever, and if you don't put into it, it could go away."

She lifted her hand to his cheek. "You snuck in that apology you said you owed me, huh?"

"If I'd have been the man you needed then, you wouldn't have had to leave me. But I'm that man now. Even sitting here in a freaking stupid chair and I can't stand up and walk with you or carry your son, I'm more man than I've ever been. Marry me and let me be Lucas's father."

"Russell, I've never wanted anything more than to be your wife, and have you as the father of my children."

"That's a yes?"

"Yes. So much a yes that I'd marry you tomorrow if it were possible."

"Come here," he urged her off her knees to face him and pressed his lips to hers. In that very moment, he knew it was true and forever love, just like what his parents had. This wasn't a wish made that came true. This was fraught with hardship and forgiveness. It wasn't even based on sex and urges. He couldn't carry her off and make love to her to seal the deal. They had to see each other for what they were at that moment. And they were lovers that never stopped loving. Obstacles kept them apart, but now they were together. He'd be damned if he'd ever lose that again.

CHAPTER 18

*E*xhaustion had the best of him, but sleep did not. Russell lay in his bed, next to Chelsea, who curled up to him. Lucas sweetly snored in his little bed.

He thought back to the Christmas he'd gotten his first dirt bike, or the one where his father had bought him his first rifle. Until that very moment, those might have been his favorite Christmas memories. All of that was about to change.

On Christmas Eve, he'd become a father. Sure, not legally yet, but it happened on Christmas Eve. The woman he'd always loved agreed to marry him, though he hadn't convinced her that a Christmas wedding was possible.

A smile came to his lips in the dark. She underestimated him and those he knew. Of course, it was midnight, but he wondered what he could accomplish.

His bedroom door opened, and a sliver of light fell over him. "Mom?"

"Oh, I didn't mean to wake you," she whispered. "Just doing some Santa duty as I'd promised Chelsea. I wanted to make sure he was asleep."

"Yeah, they're both bushed. Help me into my chair. I'm awake."

She tiptoed into the room as Russell swung his legs over the side of the bed. He balanced on his good leg as she moved his chair into place. He felt strong at the moment. That was a nice change, he thought.

His mother held his chair until he sat down and then she pushed him out of the room without disturbing either of them.

The lights from the Christmas tree illuminated the room. It was no secret that his mother would spend hours there, during Christmas, and just watch the lights twinkle.

"She had all these gifts for him?" Russell asked as he saw the presents under the tree.

"Only a few, but I couldn't help myself. I adore him, Russell. I had to add a few things. I hope she'll be okay with that." He smiled, and she noticed. "You think she'll be mad?"

"No, Mom. She won't be mad. Can you sit for a moment? I want to talk to you."

A flash of concern masked her face. She moved quickly to sit on the sofa, and he moved toward her.

"Everything's okay?"

"Everything's perfect." He took a moment to pull his thoughts together. "Last night, Lucas called me Daddy."

She pressed her hands together and put them to her lips. "That's precious."

"I've never had anything move me so much. But the fact is, I love him. I love them both."

"I know. We all love them. You know that, right?"

"I do. That's why I did what I did." He leaned in toward his mother. "I asked her to marry me, and let me adopt Lucas."

She moved in toward him. "And?"

"She said yes."

Those were the magic words that set his mother into a crying frenzy, and he couldn't even move from his chair to go to her.

"Russell, I'm so happy. Oh, you have no idea how happy this makes me."

"I have an idea." He eased back. "I asked her to marry me on Christmas—well today."

"Not very practical."

He laughed now. "That's what she said. But she still agreed. However, I have enough connections, and I'll bet I could throw a wedding today."

"You really want to do that? You can't get a license until tomorrow."

"It's not about the license. It's about the commitment. Sure, I'll make it legal, and then I'll start going forward with the adoption too."

"It's midnight on Christmas. How are you going to pull this off?"

"I'm about to text my cousins and my brothers and get this all put together. Are you with me? Will you help me?"

"Honey, this is the best thing. But you're sure you want to do this now? Her parents aren't here. You're not out of the chair and walking." She gestured to the obvious.

"This is a perfect time. This means it's all about us and nothing else."

"Anything you want. Tell me what I can do."

"Don't tell her. I want it to be a surprise. But let's make a list."

THE SUN WAS up when Chelsea opened her eyes, and Lucas was in the bed next to her, not Russell. She looked toward the door and noticed that it was closed.

She sat up and whispered, "Russell?" Wondering if he were in the bathroom, but the door was open, and the light was off.

As she stirred, Lucas sat up next to her and rubbed his eyes. He crawled into her arms and rested there. These were the moments she'd cherish forever. She never knew she could love someone as much as she loved him.

"Where's Daddy?" he asked with his voice full of sleep.

She took a breath and decided from that moment on she'd never worry about correcting him. "Let's go find him. Maybe Santa came to visit again too," she offered, hoping that Glenda had worked her magic in the middle of the night.

Knowing that she wasn't alone in the house with Lucas, she quickly dressed by finding a pair of sweatpants, a clean T-shirt, and a bra. She gave her hair a quick brushing and piled it in a knot atop her head.

Lucas stood at the door, his hand on the knob, and waited, more patiently than she would have at that age.

"Okay, let's go look for..." she sucked in a breath, "Daddy."

"Daddy!" He flung open the door and ran down the hall yelling, "Daddy! Daddy!"

They turned and walked through the kitchen, which was empty. The scent of fresh coffee filled Chelsea's nose and she wished to stop, but she followed.

He circled through the dining room and out to the living room where Glenda, Everett, Ben, Gerald, and Russell sat in anticipation.

He hurried to Russell. "Daddy!" He climbed into his lap without help. "Santa came."

Chelsea looked around the room and the expressions associated with Lucas referring to Russell as his daddy. Everett had a look of deep concern, and she couldn't blame him for that. She was sure she'd too have that same look. Glenda already had tears in her eyes. There wasn't any disappointment or concern there. His brothers, on the other hand, were bewildered.

Russell, however, smiled from ear to ear.

"Look at that. Santa did come back last night. Do you want to open presents?"

Lucas nodded enthusiastically and climbed down from his lap and moved straight for the tree.

"I need my camera," Glenda jumped up. "Give me one second, kiddo."

She moved to Chelsea, taking her by the hand, and tugging her along into the kitchen with her.

"I thought you could use some coffee. I could use some coffee. Oh, he's precious," she continued. "I hope you don't mind. I couldn't help myself. I added a few presents under the tree. I just love having him here and I..."

Chelsea moved to her and wrapped her in a hug. "Thank you," she said. "For everything."

When she pulled back, Glenda was blinking away tears that broke through and rolled down her cheek.

"He told me you said you'd marry him," Glenda admitted. "I'm so happy, Chelsea. You've always brought out the best in Russ."

"I worry that it's not me that does that."

They both turned their head when they heard Lucas squeal from the other room.

"They need each other," Glenda assured her. "He'll be the best daddy he can be to him."

"I know he will. It only makes me love him more."

Glenda pulled down two coffee mugs, filled them, and handed her one. "We should get back out there. If he's like my boys, he's going to explode."

Chelsea laughed as she followed Glenda to the other room.

The first thing she noticed was that Russell had moved from his wheelchair to the sofa. She wondered if that was even comfortable for him, sinking so low into the cushions. His leg was propped up, and he looked anything but uncomfortable. He looked at peace, and he hadn't had that look since he'd come back into her life.

"Come sit down. He's at the end of his patience," Russell patted the seat next to him and Chelsea took it.

The plethora of gifts from Santa had been torn open and glee-fully embraced within minutes. All of the precious moments were caught on Glenda's camera, and Chelsea watched it all unfold, wrapped in the arms of the man she loved.

There had never been a better Christmas, ever.

"I need to get this cleaned up and help you with Christmas dinner," Chelsea began to stand, and Glenda held a hand up to her to stop her.

"Susan is having Christmas dinner at Lydia's event hall in town. A little more formal."

Chelsea bit down on her lip. "How formal? I didn't pack anything nice. And the dress Pearl brought isn't formal, will it work?"

Glenda laughed. "That's the best part about having family in the retail business. Gia has a dress for me that she picked up in Lucca when she was there last. I can't wait to see it. I'll bet she can find you something, or even better, we can see if Pearl has something."

"I can't ask them to go to work on Christmas, so I can have something to wear to dinner."

"Yes, you can. That's what family is for," she said and hurried away.

Chelsea turned to Russell, who sat there grinning at her. "You might as well just go with it. She's not going to back down."

"I feel bad. I don't have gifts for anyone."

"Chels," he lifted her chin with his finger. "Don't you see? Your being here has been the best Christmas gift of all—for all of us."

They both turned to see Lucas holding a toy toward Everett, and Everett slid from his chair to the floor to play with him.

"He belongs here, Chels. And so do you."

CHAPTER 19

*R*ussell's mood had plummeted when Esther, the nurse Karen had said would be coming by, arrived.

It was Christmas, so her demeanor and bedside manner weren't what Karen's were. She didn't want to be there, and it showed in everything she did.

"Whose bed is this in here?" she snapped at him.

"My son's," he replied as if he'd been saying it since Lucas had been born.

"You can't rest with him in here."

"Oh, I do just fine with him in here. I'm better with him in here," he stated firmly, and Esther gave a loud humph.

He didn't like the way she directed Chelsea while they went through his physical therapy. And he was damn glad that his mother had taken Lucas out to the kitchen to play with his coloring books from Santa.

Esther was there an hour, and by the time she left, Russell was exhausted.

"Can I do something about who comes out here to train you? I didn't like how she talked to you," he groaned as he watched her pick up the room after physical therapy.

"There are only so many people who can train me, and you have to admit this is an unusual situation. I should be in a clinic, not in a private house. I get to do this because your mother had the right connections."

"I suppose, but she made me feel worse."

Chelsea smiled and moved to him. "It was one hour out of your day. It's all going to be okay now, and tomorrow you go in, and they'll look to see how you're doing. My guess is, you'll come home with a little less hardware," she joked scanning a hand over him like a magician.

"I'd be happy to have a lot less of this crap. I never thought I'd be so excited to pee on my own."

She laughed a hearty laugh at that. "That's what happens when your truck impales you. Considering that accident could have ended so differently…"

"I know. I'm lucky to be alive," his voice dipped. Russell reached for her hand. "Why do you think someone did this? Sure, I talk crap, but the way Phillip tells it, someone tried to kill me."

She cupped his face in her hands. "I don't know. It's all too coincidental with the truck having been stolen, my house having been broken into, and my ex on parole."

"Are you scared?"

She shook her head. "I haven't been since I walked in the front door of this house. I don't understand it all. All I know is I want it to end, and I want you healthy so we can start this new life. If it's all just been coincidence throwing us together again, I'll take it."

"My mom would call it fate."

"Fate then," she whispered and kissed him gently. "Tomorrow we'll talk to Phillip. He was going to study the surveillance again. Maybe he found something. We'll have him check on Dominic too, just to make sure he's still in Texas."

"And you think this will make it all go away. We're going to find out that it just happened I was run off the road in a stolen truck that had been in your garage?"

"I want to think that."

"One day at a time."

"It's what we've got, right? I should check on Lucas. He's going to need a bath before we head to town."

Appreciating the view as she walked away, he thought about the moment when he could get on the floor and give Lucas his bath and tuck him in. He could never have imagined that he would crave such things.

His cell phone buzzed on the nightstand, and he pushed himself toward it. Phillip Smythe's name appeared with a text message.

Fiona Cleary, Chelsea's ex-mother-in-law, was picked up in Athens last night on DUI. She said she'd come from Macon, which means she's been nearby. I'll need to talk to Chelsea tomorrow, and you too. I won't mention it tonight. Just wanted you to know.

He held the phone in his hand rereading the message over and over. So perhaps Dominic Cleary wasn't there, but his mother was. She'd had a hand in Lucas's kidnapping too. This wasn't sitting with him very well.

The more he thought about it, perhaps she'd have reason to have run him off the road. After all, Chelsea had broken ties with him only shortly before she left with Dominic. He texted back.

Did you run prints from the truck to match her?

He waited until Phillip responded.

Working on that. Not going to talk about it today. You have plans. I'll see you tonight.

Russell bit down on the inside of his cheek. If he wasn't going to go into it, why did Phillip bring it up? He seemed to have a habit of doing such things.

THE HIGHLIGHT of Russell's morning had been that Chelsea had given him his shower. His lewd comments and immature groping of her, while she worked, had only aggravated her, but he could read her eyes. She was merely trying to be professional, as there was no need to get sexually worked up when there was nothing they could do about it.

Once she'd helped him get dressed, she was busy elsewhere with Lucas and Russell's mother. It was a good thing, too. His phone hadn't stopped buzzing since he'd put the first text into Susan at one o'clock that morning.

Chelsea walked into the office where Russell was scoping out houses on the computer. He quickly changed over his screen to Facebook. There was no need to let her in on the house search yet. They had other things going on.

"Your mom wants me to go into town with her to pick up her dress and see if Gia or Pearl have something I could wear. I've never had a Christmas dinner so fancy I had to get a dress."

"My mom does Christmas up right."

"I know. I just..." She blew out a breath. "So anyway, Lucas and I are heading into town with your mom. Your dad, Ben, and Gerald are coming later, and you're coming with them."

"Sounds like a plan. We can take Lucas with us."

He saw her shoulders tighten. She wasn't ready for that yet, and he could understand.

"He's fine with us." She walked around behind the desk and kissed him gently, and then looked at the computer. "Facebook? You know, we're not friends on Facebook."

"You don't say?"

"Find me. Let's be friends."

He searched her name, and when her picture came up, he looked at the profile. "How old was he in this picture?" he asked of the photo of her and Lucas on her cover picture.

"He was six weeks old."

"He looks just like you."

She smiled still looking at the picture. "It was right before he was kidnapped."

Russell squeezed her hand. "He was that little?"

Chelsea nodded. "He'll never remember it, and for that, I'm grateful."

There wasn't anything he could say now. He needed to show her that she and Lucas could trust him forever.

Russell clicked on the button to add her as a friend on Facebook and a smile displaced the frown on her lips.

"I accept," she said with a laugh.

"Good. We'll change our relationship status too—as soon as you officially accept my friendship."

She laughed and kissed him again. "I'll meet you in town. Merry Christmas, Russell."

"Merry Christmas."

CHAPTER 20

$\mathcal{C}$helsea hadn't been to Gia's new store in the building of which Lydia Morgan and Pearl Walker-Morgan were the owners. She'd heard many things about it. Pearl had told her once it was a *wedding mecca,* and that it was.

There was an event center, a bridal store, flower shop, bakery, photographer, and of course Gia's gift store. It was fantastic.

The lights were on in Pearl's bridal store, but nowhere else. The sign in the window still said closed, but Glenda walked straight to the door and pulled it open.

Chelsea followed, picking Lucas up and placing him on her hip so he wouldn't touch anything.

Pearl and Gia moved to them and hugged each of them, including Lucas, who hid his face in his mother's neck.

"Girls, every time I come here, it looks more beautiful," Glenda complimented as she looked around the store. "Lydia sure has an eye for location, doesn't she?"

"It's her calling," Pearl agreed.

"And the smells from the event center are fantastic."

Gia laughed. "Susan has been over there all day cooking.

Dinner will be wonderful. I sent back cases of wine from Lucca when Dane and I were there. I took a few bottles over for later."

Glenda's cheeks rose as she smiled. "I can't wait. So, my dress."

Gia nodded. "I brought it over to steam. It is in the back."

Glenda followed Gia leaving Chelsea and Lucas alone with Russell's cousin, Pearl.

"So you need something for tonight, too?" Pearl asked.

"I've been told. I've never had a Christmas dinner that's this fancy. I'm a bit out of sorts."

Pearl's eyes were wide, and a smile grew wide on her lips. Chelsea noticed that Gia and Glenda had come from the back, a dress draped over Gia's arm. A moment later Bethany, Russell's other cousin, burst through the door with an enormous box, and her eyes matched those of everyone else.

"Why is everyone just standing here?" Bethany asked. "We have things to do."

They all shifted their eyes back to Chelsea, who could only stare at the antics going on around her. "What do we have to do?"

Bethany set the box down on the table, and they all walked toward her. When she took the lid off, she revealed an entire box of beautiful flowers.

"Chelsea, do you want pink or red roses?"

Chelsea batted her eyes. "I'm sorry. Roses?"

Bethany dropped her shoulders and looked at the others. "Seriously? You all waited for me to tell her?"

Pearl laughed. "We just figured you'd be the first one to crack."

Bethany shook her head and laughed as well. "I'm just too freaking excited."

Chelsea boosted Lucas on her hip and looked at all of them. "Is this some new Walker Christmas tradition? I'm lost."

Bethany exchanged looks with everyone else and then threw her arms up. "Fine. I'll tell her. Why didn't he do this?" She looked at Glenda.

"Just tell her."

Bethany put her hands on her hips. "Chelsea, we're here to throw you a wedding."

Her hand came directly to Lucas's back as if to protect him because she'd suddenly gone shaky.

"I beg your pardon?"

Pearl put her arm around her and guided her to the sitting area where brides would try on dresses. Waiting there was a tray of champagne and strawberries dipped in chocolate.

"We all started receiving texts at one this morning. Russell said he proposed and wanted to give you a Christmas wedding."

"It's not possible. I told him that."

Pearl nodded. "It's not possible for most people, but he has family in the business. So he's arranged for you to pick a dress with me. Bethany is putting together your bouquet. Audrey will be here in a bit to do your hair and makeup. Susan is cooking us an enormous celebration meal, and Lydia is an officiant."

"She is?"

"Yes. It made sense since she owns different event venues. It's amazing what you can do on the internet."

"I don't know what to say."

"Say you'll marry me," Russell's voice came from behind them and she turned to see him there with his father and his brothers already in tuxedos.

She moved to him, setting Lucas down on the ground, she wrapped her arms around Russell tightly. "Russ, this is crazy," she said laughing through her tears.

"Yep. I wouldn't want it any other way." He rubbed his thumb over her knuckles. "I couldn't get your parents and sister here, though. But they send their love. Your father even gave me his blessing." The tears streamed down her face, and he wiped them away. "Is that okay?" he asked.

"I love you."

"I love you, too. Tomorrow when we come to town, we'll get that license and file it. Then we'll start on adoption."

She bent down to hold him. When she was little, she'd dreamed of being a fairy princess, and her prince would sweep her off her feet. How many other girls had their dreams come true like this, she wondered?

"Come here." Russell held his arms out to Lucas as Chelsea stepped back. "You're coming with the boys," he said lifting him on his lap. "This is my best man. We have to get him dressed. I'll see you in an hour."

She only nodded, because words wouldn't form correctly to tell him how surprised and blessed she was. They'd have time for that.

PEARL HAD BEEN THINKING of the perfect dress since she'd been awakened at one in the morning by Russell's text, she told Chelsea. A new sample had arrived the week earlier, and she knew it would be the perfect wedding dress for her.

It was form fitted, off the shoulder, and white satin. Elegant without being over fancy.

Chelsea fell in love with it right away. "I never thought I'd look this good on my wedding day. I kinda thought we'd end up at the courthouse." She laughed. "And that would have been fine too," she sighed as she looked in the mirror.

"Russell would never leave it for the courthouse. Although, why he didn't want to wait until he was on two feet, I'll never understand."

Glenda raised her glass of champagne. "He said it's about the commitment. He doesn't want another day to go by without Chelsea as his wife."

Gia held her hand to her chest. "That is precious."

Glenda took a long drink of her champagne. "My boys are finally getting married. I was worried. Eric wasn't getting any younger when Susan finally came along. Now Gia and Dane are getting married. And Russell is marrying Chelsea, just as he always should have."

Chelsea smiled and swallowed hard. She wanted to take it badly that Glenda had said, *just as he always should have*, but even she'd said that too.

Bethany sat in the other room fixing up a perfect bouquet and Audrey, Pearl's sister—another one of Russell's cousins—had come by to put up Chelsea's hair and do her makeup.

Chelsea laughed as Audrey sprayed her hair in place. "I was serious when I told him this was totally impractical. I would never have dreamed he'd throw me a wedding for Christmas."

Audrey rested her hand on Chelsea's shoulder. "Don't be upset when he doesn't live up to it every year. Just keep this one close to your heart. You know how men are."

They all had a good laugh at that as they continued to ready the bride-to-be for her walk down the aisle.

<hr />

RUSSELL SAT by the door waiting for word that Chelsea was ready. His father had gone next door to check on them, and he took Lucas with him so that Chelsea could see him in his little tuxedo.

"I thought *I* lived life in the fast lane," Jake gave him a gentle slap on the shoulder and took the seat next to him. "When I came to visit you in the hospital, it didn't seem as though you two were hitting it off."

"We have a history. It just all came back."

"Yeah, and isn't she still in some trouble? Word around town is she had that truck that ran you off the road. Smythe could arrest her for that."

Russell clenched his jaw. "It was in her possession and was stolen from her. She's been in touch with Phillip Smythe the whole time. We're good here."

Jake nodded. "You're cool with the kid too?"

Russell clenched his fist to his side. "Best thing to happen to me. Him and Chelsea that is. So yeah, I'm cool with it."

Jake chuckled as he stood. "You're a good man."

As he walked away, Russell wondered how many others felt the same way. Seriously, was this such a big deal? He loved her years ago, and for the three years they weren't together, he still loved her. Now was his chance to capture that and not waste any more time.

Did it matter what his cousin thought? The man was used to just having women fall at his feet. What would happen if the great, fast, Jake Walker ever got caught? Oh, Russell would bring up this conversation, he thought. Yes. He'd question his thoughts when the man decided to get married.

The thought made him chuckle to himself. They'd always been a little competitive. Russell had the fire inside him just like Jake. Russell used his to fight, and Jake used his to race.

Only now, Russell was going to have to think about things a little differently. He had a son to raise and to mold. And that hit him. What kind of influence could he possibly have on a young mind?

Gerald walked toward him carrying the crutches he'd had in storage. "Are you sure about this?" he asked as he handed them to Russell. "You haven't done this."

"I'm not going to look up at her while I marry her. I'm going to stand like a man for the fifteen minutes I need to stand up."

"Well, you'd better be ready, because she's ready."

Russell's heart began to hammer in his chest. This was it. The day he'd waited years for. He'd done it. He'd managed to put a wedding together on Christmas Day.

CHAPTER 21

*T*he lights of the hall were dimmed, and sparkling white lights illuminated the altar where Lydia stood, and Russell waited. Chelsea stood at the back of the center, ready to walk toward him with his entire family looking on. His brothers, their wives, and fiancées watched. His cousins and their spouses. Even his uncle had come to witness the wedding, and Chelsea had heard that he'd had to *think* about even walking his own daughter Bethany down the aisle, which was some of the reason Pearl eloped.

In the corner, she saw Audrey with a cell phone faced toward her, and she knew at that moment, even her parents were in attendance via Face-Time.

Could she have fallen in love with a better man? She should never have left him in the first place, but that was water under the bridge as he'd said. This was a new beginning, and her forever.

Glenda sat in the front row of white chairs with Lucas on her lap. It looked as though he'd fallen asleep, and the thought made Chelsea giggle to herself. He was comfortable with his new family. That's all she could ever hope for.

She gave Lydia the nod, and Lydia then cued someone to start the music. Chelsea made her way toward the man she loved, who sat in his wheelchair only a few feet away. And once she reached him, she'd get her happily ever after.

His family stood as she passed them, and made her way to the altar.

Russell didn't say anything. He only looked at her. He then turned to Gerald, who moved between them. Ben held on to the chair, and Gerald helped Russell up on his good leg, and secure the crutches under his arms.

"What are you doing?" Chelsea whispered as Gerald moved away and she saw him standing there.

"I wasn't going to sit down for this. Lydia has a time frame," he joked and winked at Lydia, who nodded.

"Are you sure?"

"Yep. Today I'm out to prove I can do anything when it comes to you."

She'd promised herself she wouldn't cry, but it was bound to happen. From the corner of her eye, she saw Everett move toward her, and he handed her a handkerchief, then kissed her on the cheek.

Once her tears had been wiped, she took Russell's hand, which she noticed had been taken out of the sling, and turned to face Lydia.

LYDIA COULD HAVE BEEN SPEAKING Chinese. Russell didn't understand a word she was saying. All he could focus on was the beautiful woman to his side—his wife—his lover—the mother to *his* son.

He felt his heart rate kick up, and he willed it to slow. If he showed any signs of weakness she'd push him back into that chair, and at this moment in his life, he didn't want that.

As it was, he couldn't even take his new bride home and make love to her. But when he could, he would. It would be a night they'd never forget.

Lydia finally got to the part of the ceremony where they could exchange vows. Chelsea's eyes grew wide. "I don't have anything," she whispered to Lydia.

"Speak from your heart. That's all."

Chelsea took a deep breath and raised her eyes to Russell's. "It was Christmas when we fell in love the first time. It only seems appropriate that we're standing here now taking these vows and starting our own life—our own family. I will cherish you forever, Russell Walker. You're my soulmate, and fate must have known that."

He raised her hand to his lips and kissed it.

"Chelsea, I wanted to marry you today, not only because you said you would," he said smiling. "But to show you that I could make miracles happen for you. You're right. Fate brought us together again, and I never want another sunrise to happen without you by my side. I love you and Lucas. And I promise to be the best, most attentive husband and father I can be."

Lydia wiped a tear from her cheek and then looked at them both.

"Do you, Chelsea Quinn, take Russell Walker to be your husband?"

"I do," she replied, nearly before Lydia had finished.

"Do you, Russell Walker, take Chelsea Quinn to be your wife?"

"Oh, yes I do."

The glimmer in her eyes said she was happy, and he was happy. Nothing could ruin this union now—nothing.

"Russell, the ring."

Now her eyes went sad. "Russ, I don't have a ring."

"Shhh, we can discuss that later." He pulled a ring from his pocket and held it at her finger.

"With this ring, I thee wed," he said, repeating after Lydia and he slid the ring on her finger.

"You got me a ring." Chelsea stared down at it.

"I got it when I got you the necklace. I knew what I wanted."

Lydia began again. "By the powers vested in me by the state of Georgia, I now pronounce you husband and wife you may…"

He never heard the rest. He pulled Chelsea close to him. "Hold on to me," he warned and handed the crutches to Gerald.

"I'll never—ever let you go," she promised as he covered her mouth in a kiss that filled his very soul and gave him a purpose for his life, which he had thought he might have lost along the way.

RUSSELL WRAPPED his arm around his new bride as they lay in *their* bed with *their* son asleep in his bed, his new bear tucked up under his arm.

Every moment of this Christmas had been nearly perfect he thought as he brushed a strand of her blonde hair from her face while she slept.

The only times he wasn't full of only joy, were when he'd received the text from Phillip about Dominic's mother, and when Jake had questioned him about Chelsea having had the truck that ran him off the road.

At this point, it could all go away, and he'd be happy. He'd be walking again soon, and Chelsea would now live in the house with him until he made plans to build their house. They could even start adding to their family now. Someone set out to hurt them, but no one would ever touch them again. He knew that in his gut. No Walker would allow someone to get to them. And Phillip Smythe would have their back, too.

THE NEXT MORNING, Chelsea was on the phone bright and early. She was checking in with the nurses overseeing her training and giving them updates that should corroborate those that Karen and Esther had given. There would be a supervising nurse at his doctor appointment today too, just so they could talk to Chelsea, the doctor, and Russell. If he had his way, he'd tell them all she was overqualified, but he figured he'd better just prove to them that he was healing from his surgery, and was ready to move forward with recovery.

"Your mom is going to hold on to Lucas while we go to your appointment. They want us there a little bit early, and I'm sorry, but that's for my benefit, not yours. It has to do with the schooling," she began to inform him as she packed up a bag of items they might need for their trip into town. "I need your driver's license for the marriage license. Where is that?"

Russell stared at her for a moment. "I guess it's with the stuff I had on me at the accident."

Chelsea turned and dropped her shoulders. "You haven't seen it since then?"

"Didn't need it. When we went to buy your necklace, I used my credit at the store."

"You have credit at a jewelry store?"

"I bought a really nice watch a few years ago. No big deal."

"Uh-huh," she groaned.

"I'd ask my mother. She would have probably taken my personal things home with her."

She rubbed her tired eyes and tucked the two loose strands of hair, which had fallen from her ponytail, behind her ears.

"If we can't find it, we can't get the license."

Russell laughed. "Fine. Then we don't get that today. In my mind, I'm not married to you any less."

"I know. I know." She moved to him and kissed him softly. "I just keep thinking that if you're doing well enough, I'll have to go back to my training. I don't have much time before my boards, but it would mean having to go back."

"I can be unwell if you want me to be."

"No. I don't want that either."

"Chels, I'd sit outside every day if I had to. Honey, nothing is going to happen to you or Lucas. I think this is over for us now."

"I don't know. Phillip was acting very strange last night, and he said he wanted to see us when we were in town today."

Russell bit back the curse. "I didn't want you to deal with that yesterday," he said, and she turned quickly to face him.

"Deal with what?"

"Dominic's mom was picked up in Athens on a DUI. And she said she'd been coming from Macon."

Her face went pale, and she sat down on the edge of the bed. "She's been in town. I didn't know her well. I'd only seen her a few times, but I know I saw her."

"You didn't mention that."

"I didn't think about it. I thought I was being paranoid." She rubbed her forehead as if to ward off the stress. "It didn't look like her, well, not the way I'd remembered her. Besides, it was before all this happened."

"So why do you think it was her?"

"A gut feeling?"

He wasn't sure what to do with that. Suddenly she sounded crazy, but he couldn't think that either. The woman *had* been in Macon.

"Your training might just have to wait until later," he said as he scooted his chair toward the bedroom door. "Chelsea, your life is more important than any career choice you're making. You only need to work if you need it to be more than just a mother and wife. And before you go telling me what's involved in that job, I already know. I've seen my mother work her ass off for years. Until we know those people are out of your life, I think you should stay here and only be around others we trust. For your safety and Lucas's."

She covered her mouth with her hand. "I hate to say you're right. But I think you are." Chelsea took a few deep breaths and then stood up. "But for today, I'm your nurse, and we're going into town to see how you're doing and to get our marriage license. I'll see if your mom has your wallet. And I'll call Phillip, and he can meet us at the hospital."

"Okay," he said in agreement as he moved out of the bedroom with her following close behind.

CHAPTER 22

Going back to the hospital had Russell's stomach in a knot. He'd honestly hoped he'd seen the last of that place.

They quietly rode the elevator to the floor where the doctor's office was located. He caught sight of Chelsea in the mirrored wall. He had to admit she was one damn sexy nurse in her scrubs and white tennis shoes.

It had surprised him when he'd first seen her at the hospital, but in hindsight, it shouldn't have. She'd always had that caring, comforting side to her. Anyone in need had a friend in Chelsea.

"How did you meet Dominic?" he asked, breaking the silence.

"Seriously? You're bringing that up right now?"

He shrugged. "I just wondered."

She watched the numbers climb on the elevator. "I got that job as a receptionist at a doctor's office. I wrote you about that."

"I remember."

"He brought his brother in because he'd broken his arm, and the doctor had been the one on call at the hospital."

Russell let out a grunt. "Had he broken his brother's arm?"

"Not funny."

"Wasn't meant to be."

The doors opened, and Chelsea pushed him down the hall to the reception desk and checked him in. The supervising nurse met her at the desk and asked her to follow her, to go over a few items.

For the first time since his accident, Russell was left alone in public, and he felt vulnerable.

Perhaps he should have called Phillip and had him meet him there. At least it would have been someone to talk to.

Luckily, Chelsea came for him quickly and pushed him into a small exam room. He studied her carefully as she shut the door. Her cheeks were flushed, and her eyes rimmed red as if she'd been crying or on the verge of it.

"Everything okay?" He reached for her, but she pulled back.

"Fine," she said just as the doctor opened the door.

Russell answered all of the doctor's questions, and Chelsea gave him all the specifics on his home care, which he'd checked against the records.

He was impressed with Russell's mobility. He'd certainly made the strides they'd been hoping for, and ahead of schedule.

"I think it's time to get you situated in a boot. One you can get around in," he said as he stood.

"Seriously? I can get out of this chair?"

The doctor laughed. "I'd keep it around. But yes. Let's get you up on some crutches this week. I want you aided, not putting all your weight on your ankle quite yet."

"Never thought that would make my day," he said smiling and he looked up at his wife, but she was certainly in another world.

Russell had the long line of staples removed from his leg, x-rays, and then one of those clunky black boots fitted on him, but the big groin to ankle bandages were gone. The sling on his arm had been removed too. He was feeling more human by the moment. Of course, the moment the catheter came out, he felt like a man again.

Through every procedure, Chelsea was by his side, however, her long distant looks and silence told him something wasn't right. But they hadn't had even a moment to talk.

The nurse made him a follow-up appointment and told him that they would continue every few days with nurses visits and physical therapy for a few more weeks.

When he tried to explain that Chelsea would be there to do that, she hushed him and gathered up his paperwork.

Phillip was supposed to meet them in the cafeteria, and Russell was eager to try using the crutches, but Chelsea thought it was best if she pushed him.

He wasn't about to argue. Her eyes had gone dark, and her jaw was tight. He'd been the cause of anger like that many times. He wasn't going to poke at the beast. For once, he was on her good side.

Phillip was sitting in the corner of the cafeteria. He was in street clothes which made Russell feel bad that he was meeting them on his time off.

As they got to the table, Phillip stood and kissed Chelsea on the cheek. "Nice to see you, Mrs. Walker."

She smiled, but it was held back, and her eyes were still sad. Phillip must have noticed. He lingered a glance on her before turning his attention to Russell.

"Still in the chair?"

"Not because I want to be," he said looking at his wife, but she was somewhere else. "I've got crutches. I'll be back to normal soon. Maybe I can get to work on Lydia's house now."

That brought a smile to Phillip's face. "It's cute. Have you seen it?"

Russell laughed. "Just in pictures. You've seen it?"

"I drive by."

He was sure he did. "She hasn't invited you over to sit on the porch and have a beer."

"Maybe drive by the front porch and she could throw a beer bottle at me," he said with a laugh.

Russell reached for Chelsea's hand. "Do you want to get something to eat while you're here? You look a little out of it."

She snapped her attention to him. "No. I'm fine." She forced a smile on her beautiful lips and sat down next to him. "What did you want to talk to us about?"

Phillip sat back down. "Fiona Cleary was picked up on a DUI in Athens on Christmas Eve."

"Russell told me. She was in Macon, though?"

He nodded. "Can't seem to pinpoint her here as a resident. But yeah, she's been around." He looked at Russell. "She might have been at the bar the night you got in the fight."

Russell ran his tongue over his teeth. "She was there?"

"Surveillance is horrible. No one matches her exactly, but we all know you can change the way you look in three weeks."

"Did you find her prints in the truck?"

Phillip shook his head.

"We located a Wesley Plum from the prints on the truck. Jake knew him to be a mechanic."

"How did Jake get involved?"

"I talked to him when I went to look at the truck. Wesley Plum is a floater. Jake has hired him a time or two when they've gotten behind on jobs. He was last working at a garage about a mile and a half from Chelsea's house."

She leaned her arms on the table. "I never took that truck out. I never even opened the garage. I didn't want it. That's why I didn't care that it was stolen."

Phillip nodded and pulled his phone from his pocket. He scrolled through the pictures and then he held it up. "Recognize him?"

Russell looked at the picture, and he felt the heat of anger rush through his veins. "That's him. That's the son-of-a-bitch who was talking crap at the bar. He's the one I got into the fight with."

"I was afraid of that."

"Why?"

Phillip put the phone down. "You weren't the only fight that night. He was arrested two hours later, at the same bar, for picking a fight with the bartender. His alibi is solid. He never left the bar. He's in the footage the entire time you would have been hit."

Chelsea gripped his hand. "But his prints were in the truck?"

"First, he said he'd been working on it. But we knew it had been stolen. Finally, he said he stole it from your garage. It seems he took some tools too," he added.

Chelsea's shoulders dropped. "How did he know about the truck? Was he just looking for any open garage?"

"He said he was paid to pick it up."

"Dominic sent him?"

Phillip crossed his arms in front of him. "Dominic says he has no idea who the guy is. He said he was hoping the truck would still be around to give it to his brother. Though he mentioned, he always figured you'd sell it."

"So this guy was working with someone. Who was he with at the bar?"

"We have his shoving match with Russell on video. There's a woman that stepped in between them."

Russell nodded. "Yeah. She'd lived a hard life. I remember looking at her and thinking that."

"She never faces the camera. Swoops in and pulls you two apart."

"You don't know who she is?" Russell asked.

"The bartender said she'd never seen her. She wasn't a local."

Russell winced. "So we're nowhere?"

Phillip shrugged. "I know who stole the pickup in the first place, and he's in custody. The Cleary boys are both in custody or holding where they're supposed to be on parole. And mom is in Athens."

"Still?"

"She made bond, but they sent her to detox."

"What about the break in at Chelsea's house? Did Wesley break in there too?"

"He hasn't admitted to it."

"So we still have a break in and a hit and run."

Phillip nodded. "I'm not just going to let this go cold, Russ."

"I know. But what about Chelsea? She's going to need to finish her schooling. I can't keep her at the house forever."

She lifted her head and the stare bore through him. "Don't worry about my schooling. I've been asked to leave the program."

"What?" The word came from both men.

Russell reached for her. "What are you talking about?"

"That's what they told me earlier, when I went to talk to the supervising nurse. They feel that in my position, where I needed to leave my rotations for my own security, I'm a danger to those I care for. Also, it was unorthodox to ask for special privileges. And then, to have married one of my patients was not professional."

Russell's breath came faster, and his pulse had ramped. He pursed his lips together and exchanged looks with Phillip, who showed equal signs of anger.

"Chels, this is crap. They can't do that to you."

"Yes, they can. And they did. They've also had someone who lodged a complaint."

"Who would have complained?"

"I don't know. That's classified information," she said, and then the tears began to roll down her cheeks.

"C'mon," he said pulling her to him. "You have a million opportunities now. Door shut—window open."

"Right. Something else will come along."

"Sweetheart, you have me. For all I care you can be a full-time mother to your son."

Her eyes lifted. "Our son."

The very thought made him smile. "That's right. Our son. And we're not stopping there you know. More kids. Full house. That's enough work for you right there, and it's the most honorable career imaginable."

She kissed him softly on the lips and sat back in her chair. "Sorry, Phillip."

"No need."

"What do we do now?" she asked, in a controlled tone.

"Did Dominic have any other friends? Anyone you know?"

She shook her head. "None that I know of. He went out a lot, but I never went with him."

"How long were you together?" Phillip asked, and Russell leaned in to get the answer for himself as well.

She winced. "I met him in April. I got pregnant in May," she said, and Russell could hear her choke on her answer. "We got married in July right after I found out I was pregnant. Lucas was born in February. Shortly after that he became violent and I filed for divorce in May. I fought for full custody and they granted it to me. A few weeks later he kidnapped Lucas." Her voice trembled, and Russell squeezed her hand. "We weren't even really together a year."

It killed him to hear her go through that timeline of her life. It had been Christmas when she told him she'd be there for him. A few months later she emailed him and said she was getting married. It had crushed him.

But to know that he'd been discharged and returned home before Lucas was even born dug into his soul.

He'd fought with himself a million times to go to her and get some answers. God, if he'd just done that, maybe he could have saved her from so many things.

Phillip slid his phone into his pocket. "I'm going to get to the bottom of this. You might not be training to be a nurse, but you're Russ's nurse. Keep him in line, okay?"

She nodded and forced a smile.

"I'll see you guys at Pearl and Tyson's wedding reception on New Year's Eve, right?"

Russell had forgotten about that. "Yeah. We'll be there."

Phillip gave them a nod and walked out of the cafeteria.

"What reception?" she asked.

"They eloped. She wanted a party for New Year's Eve for her reception. I hadn't thought much about it."

"I think it's sweet that they eloped."

"With Byron Walker as your father, would you want to mess with it?"

She chuckled. "I never really thanked you for our wedding." She reached her hand to his cheek. "No one else in the world would have done something like that for me. I'm sorry that you had to go through all of this, but I'm so glad it threw us back together. I had missed you, Russell. I'm glad I never have to miss you again."

He pressed a gentle kiss to her lips. "I know the perfect way you can thank me," he said with a wink, and her cheeks filled with pink.

"Let me push you to the car. We'll get home faster that way."

CHAPTER 23

*W*hy people frowned upon marriage was a mystery to Russell. Seriously, the perks were worth every fight he knew he and Chelsea were going to have.

He'd been grateful that his mother had *wanted to take Lucas to visit Susan and Eric,* she'd said with a grin. Wasn't it also convenient that his father and brothers were busy with the cattle?

The house had been theirs for hours. He'd envisioned making love to Chelsea since the last time, years ago. And especially since he'd seen her that first day in the hospital, he'd dreamed about it every night. Of course, it certainly hadn't gone as planned.

He was still sore and bruised. Even though he was wearing a boot and not a cast, his ankle was still broken. His shoulder was stiff and didn't want to move. And, there was that little part of having just had a catheter, so some other parts were sore too.

Chelsea laughed as she rolled onto her side, her naked body exposed to him to look at and touch.

"Don't be disappointed, Russ. To tell you the truth, it's been so long for me I might have forgotten what it was like anyway. Just think, when everything works out, it'll be the best first time."

He propped himself up on his elbow and ran his finger over

her collarbone. "Damn straight. I know you remember how good I can be."

"Oh," she sighed. "I remember."

He rolled back and looked up at the ceiling. "You know, we need to find my driver's license and get that marriage finalized." He smiled. "Maybe the sex will be better then."

Chelsea laughed. "Where should I look if your mother didn't have it in your items from the hospital?"

Suddenly that came back to him. He sat up and picked up his cell phone. "Jake, where's my truck?" He nodded and listened. "I'll be there in a few hours."

"What's going on?"

"We have to go to town." He swung his legs over the edge of the bed and picked up his T-shirt. "Jake has my truck. My wallet always fell out of my pocket and got lodged in the seat. I'll bet it's there. But another thing," he said as he turned to her. "No one has mentioned my gun in the glove compartment."

"You had a gun? What were you going to do with that?"

"I'm a southern man. I keep a gun." He slowly pulled on the T-shirt. "The gun must not be there. Phillip would have said something about it."

"So, you think whoever ran you off the road took it?"

"Yes, after I crashed. It was there when I got into the truck because I took it out and laid it on the seat. I was worked up, and you never know what might happen."

"You would have shot someone?" She reached for the sheet and pulled it up over her.

"No. I would have defended myself, if they *had* come after me face to face."

"So why did they take off with it? Why not shoot you with your own gun?"

"Because I was unconscious. They figured I'd already been killed. And up until this very moment, everything has been focused on the outside of the truck. We haven't thought about the inside."

She reached out to touch his arm. "Why did someone want to hurt you?"

He shook his head. "I can't even begin to answer that. Not one bit of this makes sense. Wesley has to know something about the person who hired him. Let's go into town and check the truck. Then we'll go visit Phillip and see if he's gotten anywhere with Wesley."

AN HOUR later they were pulling into the lot of Jake's garage. The sun was low on the horizon, and the air was cold, making Russell's muscles ache as they'd never ached before.

Jake came from the garage wiping his hands on a greasy red towel. "I could have been home an hour ago," he said with a nod in their direction.

"Sure. That's not some grandma's car you're working on in there," Russ poked at him for working late on another hot rod he was building as he climbed from the truck and waited for Chelsea to bring the chair around. He'd found that even trying the crutches with his sore arm was a bitch. The chair would have to do. "When's your next race?"

"Few months. You should come. It's in Florida. Nice and warm."

Chelsea secured the chair next to him and helped ease him in.

"Okay, where's my truck?"

Jake pointed to the side of the garage, and Chelsea pushed him toward the heap of metal that had caged him in.

"Damn," he said slowly on a breath that escaped his lungs. Okay, they were right. He was lucky to be alive.

"Oh, Russ," Chelsea sobbed, and when he looked at her, her hand had come to her mouth, and her eyes were wet.

"You can go sit in the car if you need to."

She shook her head. "No. I'm fine."

Jake tucked the rag into the pocket of his coveralls. "What are you looking for?"

"My wallet often falls out of my pocket and lodges itself in the seat. I haven't seen it since I left the bar."

Jake nodded. "Okay, let me see what I can find."

He went to the truck and climbed through the window of the passenger side. Russell watched as he contorted his body in the smashed cab trying to flip the seats. A few moments later, he reached his hand out the window with the wallet in his hand.

"That's it!" Russell hollered. "Now, do you see my gun?"

"What the hell? You had your gun? Who were you going to shoot?"

Chelsea laughed. "He's a southern man. He carries a gun."

Jake nodded in agreement and went down in the cab, searching. He took longer this time, and when he poked his head out the window, he waved for them to come closer.

"You weren't shot were you?" Jake asked.

"No." Russell shook his head. "Why?"

"I would suppose that's why they didn't look for bullet holes in your cab." Confined in the small space of the crushed cab, Jake pulled the back of the seat down to reveal a bullet hole that would have been only inches from Russell's head. "Your gun isn't here."

"Son-of-a-bitch!" He turned to Chelsea. "I guess they didn't think I was dead enough."

"I don't like this, Russ." She sobbed again.

"Neither do I."

PHILLIP SAT at his desk and kept his eyes on Russell as he relayed what they'd learned. "So now we have a hit and run, burglary, and attempted murder for sure." He ran his hand over his head. "Seriously, we need some answers."

"Check the pawn shops. Maybe they tried to sell my gun."

Phillip nodded and wrote a note on the pad of paper on his desk.

"I talked to Wesley again. He admitted to knowing Fiona, but only after I showed him the picture of her. The name hadn't rung a bell. He says knows Dominic's brother, but not Dominic."

Chelsea leaned in toward the desk. "Which picture did you show him?"

Phillip turned toward his computer and typed her name. He then turned the screen toward them.

"Are you shitting me?" Russell nearly stood from his seat. "That's her! That's the woman that broke up the fight."

"The woman with the dark hair?"

"Well, yeah, but like you said, you can change your appearance in three weeks easy." He studied her closer. "I remember thinking how old she looked and how she must have had a horrible life. It shows on her face."

He turned to Chelsea, whose eyes were wide as she looked at the picture. "That's her. I did see her. She had on big sunglasses and a hat. So she didn't really strike me as her, but I felt it. I know I did."

"Okay, let me make some calls. We might have caught ourselves a break, especially if she took the gun." He picked up his phone from his desk. "Why don't you guys head home. I'll call you when I learn something."

Russell nodded. "Okay. But I think we're going to detour and get us a marriage license now that I have my wallet."

"Yep, better make that legal," Phillip joked as he dialed a phone number and waited for an answer.

CHAPTER 24

*V*ery—very—slowly, Russell managed into the county building on crutches. Not even laying in that bed after surgery had hurt as much as it did taking his first assisted steps.

"You should have waited," Chelsea said as she poised at every step to help him. "Let me go get the wheelchair. You need more physical therapy."

"Oh, this is therapy enough," he laughed as he winced at the pain.

He'd be damned if he'd roll in for the license. He'd stood for the ceremony. It seemed fitting to him.

The process took a mere few minutes. That surprised him. He was sure it would be like visiting the DMV where you wait in line for hours.

"Okay, we just need to get Lydia's signature as the officiant and two witnesses," Chelsea said as they made their way back to the car.

"Easy enough. We head to the wedding mecca and have Lydia, Pearl, and Gia sign off on our marriage."

BERNADETTE MARIE

Chelsea let out a laugh that warmed his heart. "It's a good thing you're related to everyone."

"Yep, or you'd still be planning a wedding," he said with a wink.

As expected, all of the ladies were at their stores. Gia and Sunshine, the young woman who floated between the stores as an associate, were stocking the shelves with the new wares Gia had brought back from her most recent trip to Lucca, Italy. And Pearl was helping a new bride find the perfect dress. Lydia was finalizing plans for Pearl and Tyson's wedding reception.

Chelsea had argued with him to use the wheelchair, but he wanted to show off. He wanted to let them know he hadn't been broken.

Gia had been the first to rush him, though carefully. She hugged him and kissed him on the cheek. A month ago that would have done him in. There were times he was sure Dane would have screwed it all up with Gia and he would have won. In fact, now that she was kissing his cheek, he felt nothing but sisterly love for her. Who would have known there was a bigger plan in the works?

Pearl wasn't as anxious to congratulate him, hobbling around on crutches. She had a more motherly approach, which had included her scolding him. That, he'd expected.

Lydia sat with them at a small table in the corner of the event center where she had notebooks and paper strung out.

"You don't know a D.J. do you?" she asked, as she cleared a place on the table.

Russell shook his head. "No. Can't say that I do."

"The busier we get, the more people I need in my contact list. Keep your ears open."

"Sure will," he said, with a grin on his lips. "We need you to sign this." He pushed to paper across the table toward her.

"Ah! And we're official," she said, after looking over the license and signing it. "Thanks for letting me be part of it."

"Thanks for not turning me down at one in the morning."

She laughed. "Who else would have thought to put a wedding together in the middle of the night on Christmas Eve? I couldn't tell you no." She leaned in over the table. "Are you going to honeymoon?"

Chelsea shrugged. "We haven't talked about it. Right now isn't the right time."

"I understand. I hope that there will be a time for you."

"There will be."

They thanked her and returned to the county office to file their official marriage license.

CHELSEA FELT free as they drove home. She was officially Chelsea Walker. It was an absolute dream come true. Russell took her hand as they started down the long dirt road back to the Walker Ranch.

"Are you happy, Mrs. Walker?"

She shifted a quick glance his way, and smiled. "I'm very happy."

"Everything will be normal soon. I promise."

She chuckled. "I have a feeling nothing will ever be normal with you, and that's okay."

"Why do you say that?"

"Because we are both a little hot headed."

"I'm hot headed," he said. "*You* just like to pick fights."

"Me? I don't pick fights. You..." She shook her head and laughed. "See, it's always been like this. Since we met, we'd argue over everything."

Russell reached his hand to her thigh and rubbed it sending an electric pulse straight through her. "We fight, but damn, we know how to make up," he reminded her, with his voice filled with heat.

She slapped at his hand. "I'm driving." She gripped the steering wheel with both hands and let out a long breath. "I suppose we'll need our own place soon. Your mother is sure to tire of our arguments."

"Or our making up," he joked.

"Russell!"

They both laughed as Russell leaned over the center console of the car so that his lips were poised at her ear. "You know what I hear?" His breath was warm against her skin. "We're going to have a lot of babies."

Chelsea slowed the car as they came to a grove of trees, and she pulled off the road and into them. Parking the car, she turned toward him and took his face in her hands.

"Do you still have all the same moves?" She asked.

Russell lifted a brow. "Are you saying they were good? I'm afraid to answer this question."

She eased back. "Why?"

"If I say yes, I'll assume you think my moves are old and boring. If I say no, it goes two different ways. Either I've lost it, and I'm no good. Or, you're digging, to find out with whom I've added more moves."

Now her brow raised. "I don't assume you haven't had any other women since I left you. Men cure heartbreak with sex. I know that."

"Not all of them do."

"Right." She narrowed her gaze. "What I was saying, was that the moves you had were pretty great. The car is a bit more confined than the bed or cab of a pickup, but I say we see what we can do."

"You're suggesting we have sex in the car on the only road toward the house?"

She laughed a sexy, sinister laugh. "I was until you pointed that out. We have a toddler now. When are we going to get another moment?"

His eyes grew wide. "I'll meet you in the back seat."

No one had driven on the road to or from the house in the half hour they had sex in the back seat of Chelsea's car. It had been quick, but Russell was just damned happy he'd functioned at all.

He'd be surprised if his mother didn't call him out right away. Both of their cheeks were pink, and the grins they wore told an entire tale, he thought.

As soon as they walked through the door, they heard the sound of giggling, and running feet headed toward them. Lucas ran toward the door, and Chelsea scooped him right up.

"Where's daddy's ride?"

"In the car, and he should be using it," she added. "He's trying to walk."

His mother turned the corner from the kitchen and stared at him, and then called for his father. "Everett, you have to see this."

He came from within his office. "They're letting you walk?"

"I'm moving up my own therapy," he said.

Chelsea shook her head. "He's going to hurt himself is what he's doing. But I'll admit, he's doing pretty good."

"Of course, I am," Russell gritted his teeth and bore the pain shooting through his arms from the crutches. "Now, everyone move. I'm headed to the sofa."

Lucas ran ahead and jumped on the tricycle that Santa had brought him. He zoomed around the rooms as he did the first day, and Russell grinned as he made his way to the sofa. He never thought he'd long for the sounds of a child playing, but at the moment, they seemed to be making him feel much better.

"Get situated," Chelsea ordered as she helped him lower to the sofa. "Prop your leg up. I'm going to get you some pain meds and some water."

He reached for her. "Can we do without the pain meds? Can't I just have a Tylenol?"

"Seriously. I see the pain on your face. You're overdoing it."

"Please."

She growled. "Fine. But you're stubborn."

"Did you ever expect anything different?"

She let out a sigh. "Not really. I'll have Lucas play something quieter too."

"No need. He's not bothering me at all."

In time, he figured, the look of surprise would leave her face when he said he didn't mind things that Lucas was doing. He enjoyed every moment he was around, and he looked forward to having more children with her.

Anyone who knew the circumstances of their relationship would say it was crazy. Certainly, he'd thought that a few times too. They'd only been back in each other's lives a few weeks, and now they were married and raising *their* son. But it didn't seem crazy. It seemed right.

Chelsea came back with a glass of water and his Tylenol. "I'm going to take a shower. Your mom is in the kitchen making dinner. She said a nurse came to check on you when we were out."

"I didn't think they'd send a nurse since I had my appointment today."

"Those are my thoughts, too. Your mom said she didn't seem concerned that you weren't there. She was more interested in the house. Your mom showed her around. She also checked your medications." She handed him the pills. "Maybe they sent her because they released me from my duties."

"It's okay, Chels."

"I know." She took a deep breath. "Is Lucas okay to play between you two?"

"He's fine. Go. Take a few moments to yourself."

"I love you," she said, bending to give him a kiss.

"I love you too, wife."

She smiled as she pulled away. "I like that title."

CHELSEA RAN the water in the shower and undressed. She ran a brush through her hair and scrolled through her playlist on her phone to find something to listen to. For twenty minutes, she wanted to shut out the world and be alone with the water and her music.

When she stepped into the shower, the music wasn't quite loud enough. She reached her hand out and turned up the volume. As she slid back under the water spray, she missed Phillip's text.

Dominic Cleary skipped out on his parole.

CHAPTER 25

*R*ussell lay on the sofa with his leg propped up, and Lucas was zipping back and forth with his police sirens blaring. It wasn't peaceful, but it was grand.

Every few laps, Lucas would stop, dismount, and run to check on him before heading back out on his police tricycle to save the world.

Russell closed his eyes and had nearly dozed off when he heard the doorbell, causing him to prop open an eye.

His mother scurried to the door, Lucas right behind her. She seemed to have everything under control.

He closed his eyes and muted the voices he could hear at the door.

A moment later he heard Lucas scream, and something crashed to the floor. Then it was silent. Lucas wasn't screaming. He opened his eyes, but no one came back through the hallway or the living room.

Russell sat up. He could hear the sound of a car speeding away down the dirt drive.

He looked out the window to see a silver sedan kicking up dust.

"Mom? Mom!" He hollered, then reached for his crutches. "Lucas?"

No one was answering.

He pulled himself up, secured the crutches under his arms, and took a few steps. He was wobbly. Then he knew why. Chelsea had given him those damn pain pills after all. They weren't Tylenol. Did she mean to do that?

The world grew fuzzy. He'd never reacted to the pills quite like this. He took a few more steps, and the room began to spin.

Pushing on, he made it to the front door. His mother was on the floor. There was blood on her head, and his gun was right beside her.

The world now spun out of control, and darkness began to take his vision.

CHELSEA TURNED off the shower and wrung her hair out with her hands. Seriously, she'd needed that. Sex in the car and a hot shower, that was her idea of letting the world slip away.

She took her time to dry off and use some lotion Gia had given her from her store. It smelled so beautiful.

She combed through her hair and decided to let it air dry. Looking at her limited wardrobe, she pulled out a pair of jeans and then looked through Russell's clothes. He had an ARMY T-shirt in his drawer, and with a smile, she slipped it on.

How sexy would he think that was, she wondered.

For a moment she realized how quiet the house had become. Perhaps Lucas had fallen asleep on the sofa with Russell. That would be a picture to start a scrapbook with.

She went back into the bathroom to pick up her phone.

When Chelsea opened the bedroom door, she could smell something burning in the kitchen. It wasn't like Glenda to burn anything. She hurried in and noticed that whatever was on the stove was left unattended and fried.

She turned off the stove and moved the pot. "Glenda? Lucas?"

She looked out the back window, but they weren't there. Afraid she might have awakened Russell, she walked through the dining room to the living room, but he wasn't on the sofa and his crutches were missing. Lucas's tricycle was abandoned in front of the Christmas tree.

"Russell? Glenda?" Her heart rate began to hammer in her chest. She thought she'd check upstairs.

Quickening her step, she hurried to the front hall to go upstairs and stopped cold when she saw both Glenda and Russell laying by the front door.

The scream she let out resonated in her head. Russell was in a crumpled heap on the floor, and Glenda was bleeding from the head, and there was a gun to her side.

Lucas.

Where was Lucas?

Chelsea began to feel faint. She began to scream for help. Looking at her phone, she went to dial 911, and that was when she noticed the message from Phillip.

Her heart pained, and she grabbed her chest. "No! No! No!"

She couldn't lose control now. She needed to help her husband and his mother and find her son.

Somehow she managed to dial 911, and just as the operator answered, Ben ran in from the back as Gerald ran up the ramp at the front.

She explained what was happening as Gerald went straight to his mother.

"Is she shot?" Chelsea asked, afraid of the answer?

"No. They hit her in the head with the butt of the gun." He didn't pick it up, but he looked at it. "It's Russ's gun."

Her breath came quicker now. "Ben get a towel and press it to her head," she ordered him, and he ran to the kitchen.

"Russ," she tried to shake him. "Russ, wake up."

She lowered her head to his face. His breathing was shallow, but he was alive. She pressed her fingers to his neck and made out his weak pulse. What could have possibly happened?

The sound of tires on the drive had her moving from her position and running outside. Phillip ran toward her.

"He's gone!" She gripped his arms. "He took Lucas. We have to find him."

"What's going on in the house?"

"Glenda and Russell are unconscious. Help me get my son!"

Now he gripped her and looked her in the eyes. "They told me you called 911. I've called out to all the units. They have eyes out. I'll have them block all entrances to town from out here, and I'll call every city that can be accessed from these roads. He's not going to get far. All of Georgia knows he might be headed this way."

"Might? My son is gone, and my husband is laying in there next to his mother."

"You have to calm down and tell me what's going on in the house."

She tried to take a deep breath, but it only made her dizzy. "He hit Glenda in the head with Russ's gun."

"Why did he have a gun?"

"He didn't. It was in the truck the night he wrecked. It was stolen from the truck."

"And Russell?"

"He's unconscious. As if he were drugged."

"What did he take?"

"I gave him Tylenol. I took them off the counter and…" Her eyes grew wide. "They weren't the right color," she said remembering them. "Oh, my, God! I should have known they weren't the right things. But I was talking to Glenda and she was telling me about the nurse that came today and checked his med…" The words stuck in her throat and Phillip took hold of her shoulders.

"Listen to me very carefully. I have to make a call. We'll get an Amber Alert out right away."

"Paramedics are on their way. I want you to go in and find that bottle. I'm going to attend to Glenda and Russ. Who else is here?"

"Gerald and Ben."

"Okay. You go get the bottle."

She nodded and ran into the house. Gerald had the towel pressed to his mother's head, and Ben was trying to wake Russell.

She ran into the kitchen and picked up the bottle.

The regular two-colored Tylenol had been emptied out. The pills she'd taken out were white, and she should have noticed they weren't right. She'd drugged her own husband.

She took the bottle and ran back to the front door. Gerald was still holding a towel to his mother's head, and she was moaning from the pain.

Ben had Russell lifted into a seated position, and he slipped in and out of consciousness. Phillip was on the front step on his phone.

Glenda batted her eyes and looked toward Chelsea. "She took him. She took Lucas."

Chelsea knelt down next to her as Phillip walked back through the door. "She?"

"The nurse that came earlier, when Russell was gone."

Chelsea looked up at Phillip, who winced at Glenda's words.

"I just got word that Fiona Cleary left the detox center three days ago. She just walked out."

Chelsea sat back on the step right behind her and put her head between her knees. This couldn't be happening again. She wasn't sure her heart could take it.

Russell opened his eyes and leaned against his brother. "Silver car," he muttered. "Sped away."

Phillip moved toward him. "You saw the car? Did you see Lucas?"

Russell fought to keep his eyes open. "Where's Lucas?"

Phillip looked at Chelsea, and now tears fell quickly. "Chels, we're going to find them. Eric is headed to town, too. Dane is in town, and he's driving around. Now I can tell them what to look for. All units are on the lookout, and an Amber Alert has been issued. We're going to have him back here before bedtime, Chels. I promise."

She lowered her head again between her knees. This had to be a bad dream. All she wanted to do was wake up.

here was a police officer at each end of the hospital hallway. The noises of the emergency room nearly drove Chelsea crazy.

They'd given her something to keep her calm, and she hated them for it. How could she possibly help find her son when she drugged up seated in a chair next to her husband in the emergency room?

Glenda had been stitched up, but they were going to keep her for observation. As horrible as it sounded, Chelsea was glad that she'd been hit with the gun, and not shot.

It was nearly eleven o'clock at night when Russell finally stirred. They'd given him an IV and monitored him.

"Chels," Russell said weakly as he reached for her hand. "I'm sorry." His voice was weak. "I couldn't get to them fast enough."

"I should have been there, Russ. I shouldn't have let him out of my sight—ever."

"Shhh, Phillip will find him," he promised.

She rested her head on the bed next to him, and he smoothed his hand over her hair.

Before midnight, Phillip pushed back the curtain and stepped toward the bed where Russell lay. Chelsea lifted her head.

"Did you find them? Tell me you…"

"Not yet."

Perhaps it was okay they'd given her something, she thought now. Otherwise, she was sure she'd have had a heart attack.

"The prints on Russ's gun were Fiona Cleary's."

Chelsea's hand came to her mouth to keep the sob from escaping. "She took my son."

He nodded. "We'll find them." He stepped closer to the bed. "We confirmed she was the one who sent Wesley for the truck. She was the one at the bar who broke up your fight."

Russell blinked hard. "Was she there when they arrested him?"

Phillip shook his head. "We think she might have been the one to run you off the road."

"Seeking some revenge?"

"Wesley's head was a lot clearer in the past few days." Phillip snorted. "He suddenly knew who she was and remembered her telling him about you. Seems as though when she figured out who you were, she wanted you out of the picture."

"I shouldn't have been an issue," he said, his voice clear now. "Chelsea and I weren't together."

She reached for his hand. "It was a sore spot in our marriage. I might have, on more than one occasion, mentioned to Dominic that I'd wished I hadn't left you."

She expected him to be mad, but a smile crossed his lips. "So, she was taking out revenge on me?"

Phillip nodded. "Seemed like if she could get you out of the picture, all the better. But I think her main purpose for getting the truck, was to get Lucas and head to Dominic."

Chelsea pressed her fingers to her temples. "I can't believe this is happening again."

"He'll be home soon, Chels."

CHELSEA HAD FALLEN asleep with her head on the side of Russell's hospital bed while she still sat in the chair.

Now that his head was clear, he wondered how she was even coping, because his heart was broken into a million pieces. He hated that he wasn't out there, trying to find their son. Oh, and if he saw Dominic Cleary, he'd kill the man with his bare hands.

As the nurse came in around four in the morning, she smiled at him, noticing Chelsea with her head on his bed.

"She doesn't look comfortable."

"I'm sure she's not. I'm surprised she slept at all. This has to be killing her."

The nurse nodded. "They gave her something to calm her. I guess it did the trick. They have your mom on the fourth floor." She looked at her chart. "You had elevated levels of GHB in your blood. Enough to knock you out quickly, but your bloodwork looks normal now. We're going to start your discharge."

"Thank you."

She rested her hand on his arm. "I'm sorry about your son. I'm praying for him."

"I appreciate that," he said, but he wanted to break down and cry. He wanted to get in the car and look for him. He had seen the car. He knew what he was looking for. They could be in Texas already, and the thought they might hurt Lucas ripped him apart.

He took a few deep breaths. Maybe they'd take care of him until they found him. Maybe, if Fiona were with Dominic, together, they'd do what was best for Lucas. They had to have done this to have him near, not to hurt him. Russell had to believe that.

By six o'clock, Russell was signing his discharge papers, and gratefully climbing into a wheelchair so that his wife could take him home. Phillip pushed open the curtains, as he had earlier in the night.

Chelsea ran right to him and placed her hands on his chest. "You found him. Is he okay? You have him?"

Phillip took her hands and held them in his. "Not yet. We've had sightings of the car though. I just talked to Lydia. I think you should go to her house until we have more word. You'll be close by then."

They both nodded. At that same moment, Chelsea's phone rang in her pocket. She quickly pulled it out and looked at the number.

"I don't know who this is," she said, and Phillip moved in.

"Answer it."

"Hello," she said with her voice shaking. Russell watched as her eyes grew big, and tears began to stream down her cheeks. "He's okay? Tell me he's okay. Where are you? I want my son back!"

Her breath shook, and her chest heaved. Phillip took her shoulders and guided her to the chair behind her before taking his phone out.

She hung up and looked at them. "It was Dominic. They are at my house and..."

"Get the son-of-a-bitch," Russell fired off.

"Wait!" she yelled, and heads turned. "Phillip, he has Lucas. He has his mother restrained. He doesn't want to scare Lucas so he wants us to go to the house and get him."

Russell shook his head. "This sounds like an ambush."

Phillip nodded. "We'll be careful. This is what we deal with. I'll be in touch."

"No," she said again. "He said I need to come. Phillip, I trust him. You didn't hear his voice. If he said he's going to give me Lucas..."

"You trust him?" Russell fixed his stare on her. "How in the hell can you trust him? You're crazy."

"I have to. My son's life is on the line."

"Our son, and what's he going to do if this is an ambush, and Lucas loses you?"

"I have to go."

Phillip stepped in closer. "Let's go. Both of you in my car. I have units moving into place right now. No one is getting hurt today."

CHAPTER 27

*A*s was the way of the Walker family, Russell noticed that everyone was there to rally for them. When Phillip drove down the street leading to Chelsea's house he saw the trucks that belonged to each of his brothers, and Gia's car. Jake and his brother, Todd, stood on the corner a block away, and just beyond them—their sisters, Pearl, Bethany, and Audrey stood on the next corner.

Pride swelled in his heart. If the son-of-a-bitch tried to flee, he'd feel the wrath of a Walker revenge.

Phillip pulled up in front of the house and turned on his spotlight. Two other police cars pulled up on either side of him and pinned him in.

He turned to Chelsea in the back seat. "Do you have that vest on?"

She nodded.

Russell winced at the thought. "I don't like this. Let me wear it and go for him."

Phillip shook his head. "He wants to work with Chelsea. You can't even walk that far."

Oh, but he would, he thought.

"I don't have any plans that she's walking into that house. If he called her, he wants this to go down well, right?" Phillip reasoned. "Call him," he told Chelsea.

She pulled her phone out of her pocket, turned it to the speaker, and redialed the number he'd called on.

"Chelsea, are you with the cop?" Dominic's voice rang out in the car, and Russell bit back everything he had not to go off on the man.

"I'm here. I want my son, Dominic." Her voice had risen with anger.

"You'll get him. Let me talk to the cop."

"I'm here, Dominic," Phillip said in a stern, calm voice.

"Listen. I don't wanna get shot. I broke parole in Texas."

"I know."

"Yeah, well I did it coz I knew my mom was going to go after Lucas."

Phillip exchanged glances with Chelsea. "She told you?" he asked.

"Yeah. She was going to head to me in my truck, but she said she hit something."

"She did," Phillip kept him talking. "Is your mother with you now?"

"Yeah," he said and they could hear her yelling at him. "I have her tied to a chair in the kitchen until you take her in. Listen, like I said, I wasn't in on this. My mom has lost her mind I tell ya. Lucas is pretty scared."

Chelsea covered her mouth and squeezed her eyes shut.

Dominic continued, "She didn't hurt him. You need to know she just wanted to be with him. She figured it was our turn to take care of him, but this ain't the way to do it."

Phillip rested his hand on her shoulder before speaking again. "Do you have any weapons?"

"Just one. It's a gun. It's not mine," he clarified. "I took it from her when I ambushed her."

Phillip's eyes widened. "You ambushed your mother?"

"Yes, sir. I don't want to be the one in trouble here, and I don't want the kid hurt."

"Did your mom hurt him?"

Russell took Chelsea's hand and gave it a squeeze. He was fighting everything he had inside him not to run into that house.

"No. She would never hurt him. She's always thought she should raise him and not Chelsea. She's not right, sir. But she wouldn't hurt him."

"Okay, Dominic, let's make a plan. I have armed police out here, and they'll do what I tell them to. Now, they have to take you in since you broke parole."

"I know. Like I said, I did it so she wouldn't hurt the kid."

Russell winced every time he called him *the kid*.

"Where is Lucas?"

"I put him in his crib and shut the door. He's crying a lot."

"And your mother is in the kitchen?"

"Yes, sir. Tied to a chair."

He motioned for officers to walk toward the car. Nearly silently, he instructed two officers to go to the bedroom and directed the other two to the back of the house, to the door to the kitchen.

"Dominic, I have my men instructed not to shoot. I want you to walk out of the house with your hands on your head."

"I want to see Chelsea first. I want to know she's here."

"We don't want to see her hurt, Dominic."

"No, sir. I would never hurt her—again. This is for Lucas's sake. I don't want him going to anyone else. Like I said, he's scared."

"I'm going to step out of the car with the phone. Chelsea will be right behind me."

Russell stepped out of the car, opened her door, and she slid out and stood next to him.

"Okay, I have Chelsea. Now I want you to come out with your hands on your head."

"I need to get Lucas."

"No," Phillip kept talking to him. "Lucas will be fine. Come on out."

"Okay," he said, and they heard the phone drop.

CHELSEA'S HEART had stopped and so had her breath. She waited for a shot to come from the door and hit her in the chest where she wore the vest, but she wasn't so sure it would protect her.

The door opened, and the lights from the cars flooded the doorway.

Dominic Cleary walked out, just as Phillip had told him to, with his hands on the top of his head. He walked to the middle of the sidewalk, lowered to his knees, and then to his chest.

Three officers ran to him, cuffed him, and moved him toward a waiting car.

He turned his head and looked at her. "She's crazy, Chels. I never would have done this to him," Dominic called out as they put him in the back of one of the other cars.

A few moments later his mother was brought through the front door with two officers who struggled with Fiona Cleary. Her hands were cuffed behind her and she fought against the officers.

"She shouldn't have that baby," she hollered and it twisted in Chelsea's gut. "She's the one that stole him from us."

The officers took her to the other waiting car.

Phillip handed Chelsea her phone. "I'm going in for Lucas. Keep that phone with you. I'll pick up Dominic's inside. Lucas is going to want to hear your voice."

Chelsea stood there behind the car door, and Russell moved, and slid out of the car to stand behind her.

208

She listened as Phillip entered the house. Then she heard him pick up the phone. "Are you there."

"Yes. Is he okay?" she sobbed into the phone.

"I don't have him yet. I'm walking down the hall to his room."

She could hear him screaming for her, and it was tearing her heart into pieces.

"I'm opening the door and turning on the light," he said, as the light in the room illuminated and she could see his shadow from outside. "Lucas, I'm here to take you to your mommy," she heard him say, and a moment later she could hear him cry into the phone.

Russell wrapped his arms around her waist and pressed his chest into her back. She could feel his sobbing as his body jerked next to her.

A moment later, Phillip walked out of the house with Lucas in his arms.

Lucas hid his face in Phillip's neck as he walked toward the bright lights.

Without thinking, Chelsea ran from Russell's protective arms and straight to Phillip. Lucas lifted his head and jumped into her arms.

"Oh, my baby. My sweet baby," she cried as an ambulance pulled up in front of the house.

"We have to take him to the hospital to have him checked out," he said.

"He's fine. Can't I take him home?"

Phillip turned her to him. "Chels, we have to examine him. Anything could have happened, even though Dominic gave him up that easy. Let's be real, okay?"

She nodded and started to the ambulance.

. . .

RUSSELL WATCHED as Chelsea climbed into the back of the ambulance with Lucas and the doors were closed. Damn, he didn't even have crutches.

A few minutes later Phillip came back to the car and those members of his family who had kept a vigilant circle, walked toward him as well.

"What's going on?" he asked, as Phillip moved in.

"They have to take Lucas to the hospital and check him out."

"He hurt him? The son-of-a-bitch hurt him? I'll kill him."

Phillip shook his head. "No. He doesn't appear hurt. Just because Dominic gave him up that easy doesn't mean Lucas is out of the woods. We'll know in a few hours."

"I want to go to them." Russell pleaded.

"C'mon," Lydia's voice broke through the crowd of family. "I'll take you. I'm parked the closest."

Russell nodded. "I'll need help getting over there."

A moment later he felt his body leave the ground as Eric and Gerald picked him up and carried him to Lydia's truck.

By the time they got him in the seat, she was climbing into the other side and revving the engine.

"Buckled? Let's go," she said, as she sped off down the street leaving the horror behind them.

The hospital was only a few minutes away, but as the sun peeked over the horizon, Russell felt the pain of the drive and wished they could get there faster.

"I hope he's okay," he muttered, and Lydia reached for his hand and held it.

"He's going to be fine. Phillip knew what he was doing, and he was scared to death for him. There'll be a wrath to pay if anyone did harm him."

"You knew what was going on, right? I mean, he said we were going to your house when we left the hospital. He said he'd talked to you."

She nodded as she turned down the next street and gunned

the engine to go faster. "I don't like the man. Despise talking to him. But when he rings my doorbell at five in the morning, I assume he's not there to harass me."

"You should give him a chance," Russell pleaded on behalf of his friend.

"No way in hell."

THE WAITING room in the emergency department was full of Walkers.

Russell took what strength he'd had left to wheel himself out to the room and address his family. Dane walked in just as he came through the door.

"Mom's doing great," Dane said. "They might let her go in a few hours. So I'll stick around and make sure they get home okay." Gia moved to him and wrapped her arms around him.

Russell looked at his cousins and brothers. They were all weary from the night before.

"Lucas is okay. He doesn't even have a scratch on him."

He saw Lydia clasp her hands as if a prayer had been answered, and Bethany put her arm around her and pulled her close.

"We're staying for observation. Nothing physical was done to him, but..."

Gerald moved in and hugged Russell. "Best to make sure."

Pearl and Tyson moved to him, and each hugged him. "So Dominic broke parole just to save his kid?"

"My kid," he corrected. "And yes. Seems he didn't want that on his conscience."

Pearl kissed his cheek. "You get some rest. We're going to postpone the party too. Until you're all on your feet again."

"Oh, no. You denied these women a wedding. You'd better

keep the party. Besides, I think we're all ready to celebrate and put this behind us."

Tyson rested his hand on Russell's shoulder. "If you're sure, then New Year's Eve it is."

CHELSEA WAS DRESSED in a new dress which Pearl had brought for her, and Russell thought that every day she got sexier.

He stood as she walked out of the bedroom and toward him and Lucas, who were dressed alike because Lucas wanted to look like his daddy.

"You two are handsome," she said, scanning a look over them.

"Two cutest men at the party," Russell laughed as Lucas ran to her, and she scooped him up.

"I'll be the luckiest girl there."

Russell pulled the crutches up and tucked them under his arms. It certainly had been a week from hell, but he was happy to be going out to celebrate with his favorite two people. This new year certainly was going to start off being his favorite one.

EPILOGUE

The air had the crispness of winter to it, but the freshness of spring. Russell held his wife in his arms as their feet dangled from the back of the pickup truck on their corner of Walker Ranch. Lucas ran back and forth in the bed of the truck, pretending to ride a horse.

Russell let out a cleansing breath as he took in the sight of their new house being secured onto its foundation.

"Do you think it's big enough?" Chelsea asked.

"Three-bedroom house. What more do we need?"

She shrugged. "I just see all this land and think big."

He kissed her cheek. "I see a smaller house and all this land that is big. Lucas will grow up here with room to run, play, grow. If Susan and Eric ever get off their asses and have kids, they can run back and forth between houses."

She laughed at that. "Their house isn't close enough for that."

"Sure it is. They can ride horses or bikes," he offered. "Trust me."

She rested her head on his shoulder. "I thought this dream had passed me by. I can't believe I'm here now with you."

"It's where you always belonged. Just like my mother said, it's fate."

"You know what'll be nice? Next Christmas we'll have our own tree."

"We could cut our own," he offered.

"Lucas and I already know what we're getting you for Christmas."

Russell laughed as Lucas ran toward him and climbed on his back. "You know what I'm getting for Christmas? That's months away," he said, toying with his son.

Lucas nodded and then wrapped his arms around his neck.

"We're giving you a baby sister."

Russell laughed. "You're giving me a…" He stopped and thought about what Lucas had said.

He turned to Chelsea, who was smiling wide, and her eyes lit with love. Then he turned back to Lucas. "You mean you're getting a baby sister?"

"Uh-huh, but I want a baby brother," he said before riding off on his imaginary pony.

"Chels, we're having a baby?"

"Yeah, we are," she confirmed as she pressed her head to his. "I'm extremely fertile. You're going to want to make sure you get fixed when you're done having babies with me," she joked, and he let out a hearty laugh as he climbed down from the truck and pulled her to her feet.

"You're right. We might need to add to the house," he said. "A baby. I think I might be in shock."

"You're happy?"

"Can't imagine I could get any happier." He pressed a kiss to her lips. "My mother is going to cry."

"Well, Susan and I will tell her at the same time, then."

Now his eyes grew wide as he stared at her. "Susan?"

She shrugged. "I guess it's time each branch of the Walker family started to grow."

He pulled her close and held her. He was right. This might just be the best year ever—for all of them.

We hope that you enjoyed reading
Walker Revenge
By Bernadette Marie
Please enjoy this excerpt from the next book in the
Walker Family series.

Victory
The Walker Family Series - Book Six

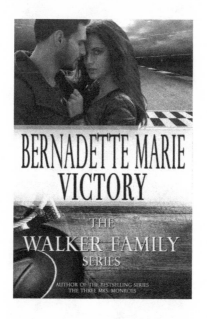

VICTORY

Georgia summer beat down on Jake Walker's neck as he ripped his helmet off his head and climbed from the race car which had slammed into the wall.

The yellow flag of caution waved as his crew ran toward him. The other cars slowed, and it always made him feel as though he were trapped on the highway with busybody onlookers trying to get a glimpse of an accident.

But when the bright pink Chevy passed by, he knew the grin of the driver was hidden behind that equally bright helmet. God, she was a pain in the ass.

"Holy hell, Jake." His crew chief Bud ripped off his cap and wiped the bead of sweat from his brow with his sleeve. "Get 'er moving," he hollered to the crew as they maneuvered the car from the wall and pushed it toward pit row.

It wasn't the end of the car, Jake thought, as he examined the damage running behind them. But it sure as hell was the end of the race. And didn't that just piss him off royally?

As his team cleared the car from the track, he turned to see the race resume and that damned pink car pulled into second. She didn't deserve to be that close to the lead, he thought. Missy

BERNADETTE MARIE

Sheridan was a princess with an attitude. The sport didn't need her.

Her daddy paid for her car and her body paid for the entry fee.

Running his fingers through his damp hair, he shook the thought from his mind. That wasn't fair to her. That was rumor and of course it circulated in a male dominated sport. But damn it, he was pissed at her, so he'd let it stir in his head that she didn't belong.

The fact of the matter was she'd pushed him out of three races now, and it was getting old. She was a damn good driver and oh what a looker. But she had a mouth to go with that driving skill, and most of the men on the track didn't take to it.

As soon as she was pushing her beast to the back of her truck, he'd be right there giving her an ear full. This wasn't going to be a habit, him being run off the track by some broad in a pink car. No, sir. She was going to rue the day she started crap with him.

MISSY WATCHED as Jake Walker's team loaded up his car. It had been a fine car she thought as she eased hers behind the leader for the next few laps.

The vibration from the speed and the roar of the engine made her whole body come alive. It was no wonder word around the track was she'd slept her way into the race. But it was the race which was her lover and gave her more pleasure than any man could.

As she turned the corner, she saw the sign she'd been looking for. The white flag was up, and this meant she had to make her mark.

Missy focused on team Justice's car. She got Walker out of the way, now Justice needed to step aside.

The engine revved as she pressed it to go faster, shifting into the next gear and pulling to the inside of the track.

Justice moved to block her, and she quickly adjusted to go high and pass him—but he countered.

Fine, she'd try again. This time, she'd aim high and see what he did.

Taking the next turn, she poised to pass him on the outside, but the red car in front of her mocked her and kept on course as a green car moved in next to her.

"Damn it!" she hollered.

"Missy, what the hell are you doin'?" Her brother's voice crept into her ear. "Maverick is pushing you out. Get the hell out of there."

"What do you think I'm doing?" she grunted as she gripped the steering wheel tighter on the third turn.

Her mother would have warned her that karma was a bitch. She'd forced Walker out of the race, so now Maverick was going to secure Justice a win by pushing her out.

Judging the gap between herself and Justice, and Maverick and the wall, she gunned the engine and pushed the car as hard as she could.

She would take Justice going on the outside.

Just as her bumper cleared the back end of his car, Maverick moved in right behind Justice.

With every foot traveled, they pushed her closer and closer to the wall. She gritted her teeth and gripped the steering wheel tighter.

Just as the checkered flag came into view, she felt the slightest nudge from Maverick's car which caused her to lose what little control she had. The front end of her car hit the wall and ricocheted her back onto the track backward barely missing Maverick.

The world was spinning now, and her brother's voice was buzzing in her ears as her car turned from the wall, through the cars on the track, and hit the grass before flipping and landing on its wheels.

. . .

JAKE WATCHED as the accident unfolded before his eyes. Oh, he'd have wanted her to lose, but not like that he thought as he and Bud ran toward her car along with her crew and the emergency personnel. Just as he drew closer, the engine burst into flames, and he could see her trying to work her way out of the car.

How he made it faster than the rest of them, he'd never know. But he was standing at the side of the car ready to aid her in getting out.

"My foot is stuck in the harness," she hollered through her helmet.

Jake managed to get her arm around his neck and hold her as she kicked free from the harness and he pulled her from the car just as they got there to put out the flames.

When her feet hit the ground she stumbled, nearly taking Jake down with her. But in an awkward dance, as people rushed past them, they managed to balance.

She quickly pulled her helmet off and looked at the car.

"Son-of-a-bitch! Look what they did to me." Her voice was lost in the bustle of chaos around them.

"Son-of-a-bitch is right." He laughed. "Karma huh?"

She spun to face him, and her long dark braid nearly caught him in the eye. "Don't start with me Walker. What are you, my mother?"

"Oh, it's okay for you to wreck me out of the race, but..."

"Don't go there." She dropped her helmet to the ground and moved in toward him.

"Oh, I went there." He firmed his stance as she shoved at him.

"You're an ass!"

"And you're a..."

Bud came between them and pushed them apart. "Now the two of you stop it. You're acting like spoiled brats. You both deserve what you got. Now kiss and make up."

Missy's eyes grew wide, and she stooped to pick up her helmet. "I'm guessing his mouth is tainted from track trash."

"And what about you?" Jake countered as Missy walked away from him, her helmet tucked up under her arm.

Bud pushed him in the other direction. "You two should just go to bed with each other and get it over with."

"What's that supposed to mean?"

"It means the tension between you both is always so thick it's like a wall."

Jake snorted a laugh. "Trust me. I don't want any part of that."

"Sure you do. Everyone does."

He supposed he couldn't blame everyone. She was a hot little number, which he verified as he turned and looked at her with her crew.

In stature, she wasn't a giant, but in attitude, she could hang with the big boys. And when she wasn't in racing gear, those legs were firm and tan. He'd often thought of running his fingers through those long brown stands of hair, but usually, in the end, he figured he'd just give them a good yank to give her pain. The thought made him chuckle. Bud was an idiot saying there was sexual tension between them. There was animosity and a competitive streak, but sexual tension—nah. Bud was a dreamer.

Jake headed back to his truck where his wrecked car sat. Maybe he'd head to the bar and find him some sexual tension. He could use some of that and an ice cold beer.

MEET THE AUTHOR

Bestselling Author Bernadette Marie is known for building families readers want to be part of. Her series The Keller Family has graced bestseller charts since its release in 2011. Since then she has authored and published over thirty-five books. The married mother of five sons promises romances with a Happily Ever After always...and says she can write it because she lives it.

Obsessed with the art of writing and the business of publishing, chronic entrepreneur Bernadette Marie established her own publishing house, 5 Prince Publishing, in 2011 to bring her own work to market as well as offer an opportunity for fresh voices in fiction to find a home as well.

When not immersed in the writing/publishing world, Bernadette Marie and her husband are shuffling their five hockey playing boys around town to practices and games as well as running their family business. She is a lover of a good stout craft beer and might have an unhealthy addiction to chocolate.